Ver
Mars

The

True

Physician

I AM
UNVEILED
BOOKS

© Copyright 2013 Verona Marshall
Published by I Am Unveiled Books
Email: info@iaubooks.co.uk

ISBN: 978-0-9927896-0-2

Publishers note: The characters in this book are fictional and do not represent any person(s) alive or dead, even if there is a resemblance. They were created solely to serve the purposes of this book. The events described in the story (which an individual may or may not be able to relate to and/or identify with), have been used as an example of a pre-cursor to embarking on a real relationship with Jesus Christ, and to highlight the truth and reality of the Gospel of Jesus Christ.

Editorial note: For grammatical concerns we have chosen not to use capitals in the name satan.

Printed in the United Kingdom

To my beautiful daughters,
You will know the truth and it will make you free.
So fear God and LIVE!

Mummy loves you xx

Contents

ACKNOWLEDGEMENTS

To The lifter of my head. My Saviour. The One and Only God - Jesus Christ. The one in whom I live and move and have my being. This is YOUR book. I am grateful and humbled to be the vessel you chose to use. Thank you.

To my daughters, thank you for giving me the inspiration and drive to be a better person. Mummy loves you.

Mum. Thank you for raising me with the values and tenacity that you did. I wouldn't be who I am, otherwise. In awe, I have watched you be resilient and humble through many trials in which many would have crumbled in. Thank you for giving me that example. Love you.

To Pastor Peter Nembhard. Thank you for giving me that push I needed to 'Step outside the box'. It's changed my life.

Nads. My big sis. From childhood you have protected me and always believed in me. Your love, prayers, and words of encouragement have meant more than I can express. Love you. You're the best.

Tilly. You never gave up on me did you girl? Your consistency, love, genuineness, and support have been indescribable and rare. Love you like cook' food.

Reverend Jacqueline Peart. Thanks for your guidance, advice, words, and continuous support. I am forever grateful.

Melanie Hamilton. Your time, support, honesty, love, and counsel mean more than I can say.

Concia Albert. Thank you for your eyes, ears, and simply just being you.

FOREWORD

It is my privilege to write this foreword for Verona Marshall - A creative, gifted, and articulate author. She is a beautiful butterfly who has gone through her own metamorphosis and has come out with beautiful colours that she shares exuberantly wherever she goes.

This fictional story* draws you into a place that will cause you to evaluate your emotions, actions, and reactions to the various obstacles that life inevitably brings. Verona's writing style is authentic and direct, opening you up to something new. Like me, you may laugh, cry and reflect as you stand in the shoes of the main character.

I have learnt first-hand that life is one of the greatest educators, *if* we are willing to learn from our mistakes as well as others. A few years ago following several major life altering experiences, I was heading down a road void of hope. However, at the end of this road I found hope when I gave birth to my passion and purpose – 2nd Chance. Every opportunity is now used to share my story and offer love. Being transparent with others is vitally important to me, especially the young people, as it helps prevent the same mistakes being made over and over again.

My biggest lesson from this book is not to write people off solely on first impressions, as maybe, just maybe, you could be the life line that they are looking for; and they may have something to offer that could enrich your own life also. Let's not forget the Word of God (The Bible) that is constant and relevant throughout this book. Each scripture used will challenge, change, encourage, or uplift you.

This book can also be used as a training resource or a tool to encourage. It's a story that, like me, you will read over and over again. A definite must read.

Melanie Hamilton
Visionary/Director
2nd Chance - London, England

*See the publisher's note on the copyright page

PROLOGUE

"You know what, Jenny? I've got one thing, and one thing only to say to you. If he's not treating you *better* than *I* treat you, which is like a queen, then he's not good enough for you. That's the bottom line."

Jenny quickly attempted to reply in her defence, but instead she paused for a second, stared out into nowhere, and pondered on her father's words.

"You know what, Paps? ... It's true. It's reaaaaally true."

Jenny then had another thought and insisted on questioning her father's previous words of advice. "I hear what you're saying Paps but what about my -"

"Don't even go there," Trevor interjected in a serious tone. "You're *gorgeous*. How many times do I have to tell you the same thing, Jenny? You're too hard of hearing."

She nodded and smiled, and nodded some more, as her father's words began to digest in her mind. As her stomach began to rumble, it reminded her that it also needed something to digest, and she snapped out of deep thought.

"Anyway, I think I'm gonna shoot off now. I'll see you later, Paps. Thanks for the chat."

She gave Trevor a big hug and kiss. Trevor smiled, exhaled deeply, and leaned back into his chair feeling pleased and reflective. He laughed to himself as he watched his daughter grab her car keys from the table, and gleefully stroll towards the front door with a smile on her face as big as the moon.

"Thanks again, Paps," Jenny shouted. "Oi, Joel, stay out of my room please and, Nats, come on! I'm starving, girl, let's go!"

"Alright, love, keep your shirt on," I snapped. "KFC ain't going nowhere you know, Jen. Take care, Trevor. Laters, Joel."

I was slightly irritated because she interrupted my train of thought. I was too busy observing them both and reflecting. I was too busy wondering why nine times out of ten, when I saw Jenny and her father hug, he always embraced her like he was never going to see her again.

Gosh man... she's only going out for some chicken and chips, Trev'. No need to get all emotional.

Okay. Maybe I shouldn't have been thinking like that. I actually really liked Trevor and still do up to this day. I have a lot of respect for him. I just think it's hard sometimes to relate to something that you've had absolutely no experience of. Trevor was a fantastic father and he still is. As for mine? Well let's just say, he's not around. Apparently, he left my mum when she was pregnant with me and shacked up with the friend who set them up in the first place. My memories of my dad are vague. I'd seen him a few times in the past, but it had always been just me and my mum.

Watching Jenny and her father always brought up a mixture of bitter and sweet emotions for me, but nevertheless, I was intrigued. Of course I was happy for my friend, but if I'm honest, I was always a little bit jealous at the same time. As far as I was concerned, Jenny had in her life what was missing in mine. Once again I found myself wondering the same thing I'd wondered a million times before. I wondered how different my life may have been, if my father chose to be an active part of my life. Watching Jenny talk about her guy troubles with Trevor... watching her hang on to every word he uttered made me ask myself, what if that was *me*? Would I have made different choices when it came to my relationships? Would I relate to men differently? Would I have felt differently about some things? Who knows? They were questions that only God could answer. The question I needed to answer right then, was to a very frustrated Jenny, who was now outside with her rumbling stomach, beeping her car horn like a mad woman, demanding to know why I was taking so long.

"Oi, Nats, bring my make-up bag, girl!" Jenny shouted from the car.

"Jenny, we're going to eat greasy chicken. Why do you want make up?" I hollered back at her, dumbfounded.

Jenny looked at me with a facial expression that I couldn't be bothered to challenge, so I reluctantly picked up her make-up bag, left the house, and approached the car - but not without getting the last word.

"You don't even need this, Jen! When are you gonna stop the obsession? You know you could be a spokeswoman for Maybelline at this rate, innit?" I joked.

"Whatever, Nats."

Jenny was contemplating her future. She had spent the last two hours speaking to her dad about Gavin, trying to work out if he was worth her while. It had taken that long because her older brother Joel kept butting into the conversation, adding his unhelpful suggestions.

"That guy is a fool!" he kept saying. The *real* truth was that *anyone* was a fool if they wanted to get together with his little sister, and all this did was wind Jenny up. After receiving words of wisdom from her dad, she'd decided to take a trip to KFC and the local off-licence so she could stuff her face, drown her sorrows, and seek my advice (which I wasn't sure was actually needed after her talk with Trevor). I vividly remember the night when Jenny and Gavin met.

It was on Jenny's birthday, one year previously, and we went out to a club to celebrate. Jenny had seen Gavin around quite a few times, but hadn't shown him much attention. In fact, she'd been playing hard to get for months. That night she finally gave in, put the guy out of his misery and gave him her number. I remember it clearly. It was me and my girlies. There was Jennifer (Jenny to all of us), Shivon, Esther, and me; and we were at our usual raving spot. The place was packed out with people. The atmosphere, vibe, and behaviour of the people were the same as always; way too much bravado, and chips the size of a continent on everyone's shoulders. You had the females walking around giving bad looks to other females who they had never even seen before, and guys walking around the place wearing designer clothes with prints so outrageous, they were an assault on the eyes. I mean, the logos and designs were virtually screaming at you. I specifically remember one group of guys who were always at this raving spot when we were there. They also loved to pose, and on this particular night, they strolled past us with their super slick fresh haircuts, big fat cheesy grins and designer sunglasses. It's a shame that they couldn't read my thoughts:

Sunglasses? Why would you do that? Are you for real? It's dark inside here! Can you even see where you're going? What a bunch of jokers…

Anyway, on this particular night we spotted Gavin calling Jenny over. We were on one side of the venue near the exit, and he was all the way over the other side, yet he managed to spot her through the masses of people. When we saw him looking over, we began to jokingly nudge Jenny, but not make it look obvious at the same time. Then Jenny said stubbornly, trying not to smile, "You know what you lot, I ain't even feeling him you know. I'm not on it; and anyway, it's blatantly obvious that I make more papers than him, so why should I waste my time?"

We weren't convinced, but decided to play along with Jenny's little game. We just smiled and said, "Oh is it, Jen?" Then we burst out in laughter while we watched her slyly touch up her lips with the lip gloss that never left her sight, as she began to walk straight in Gavin's direction to supposedly "go to the toilet". It was obvious to us all, that it would have been much quicker for Jenny to take the usual and quicker route to the toilet, rather than to walk purposely in Gavin's direction, but hey - that was Jenny for you.

After a few hours of dancing, laughing, and trying to talk over loud music, the night started to take its toll on me. I was the dancer out of all of us. I could go on and on for hours. I loved to dance and had been this way since I was a child, but even *I* knew when I needed to take a time out (well usually anyway). Esther and I slothfully strolled to the bar to get a drink, and I could see that she was tired as well. My suspicions were confirmed when she ordered a Red Bull.

"I think I'm gonna make a move soon you know, I've got a dissertation at home with my name on it so I need some sleep," Esther said, yawning like she hadn't slept for a century. Her yawn was so full on that I could see her tonsils and all sorts going on at the back of her mouth. I never realised it was humanly possible to open your mouth that wide until that moment.

"That's cool, girl," I said, "This place is a bit dry tonight anyway."

Esther was cool. She was always up for a good night out but could never last the distance. She was a typical homebody, and would rather be at home with Mark or getting sleep so she could wake up early and get her head back in her books. Esther and Mark had been together for years. They made such a nice couple. I could never envision them splitting up. Up until that point in my life, they were the only couple I knew that hardly had any drama in their relationship.

We both sat there sipping on our drinks, looking around for Shivon. Esther tiredly slid off the stool at the bar and stood up before making her suggestion.

"You check the toilets, and I'll check where the DJ's are, and let's meet back here in ten."

"Cool, Ess," I said. "I'm telling you girl, she better not have been popping any E's or nothing, 'cause I'm not in the mood for the hype. She needs to calm down."

That was the usual. Shivon would always wander off and not tell anyone where she was, especially when she'd been taking drugs. We'd all begin a tiresome search through the club, which would result in one of us finding her either throwing up in the toilet, or making a big attempt to scrape the wallpaper off the wall in some corner, dancing with some guy she'd just met. In this case it was the latter. I just smiled to myself and sighed as I watched her.

This girl is definitely one of a kind.

I heard a song that I liked, and although I was tired, I began to dance. I couldn't help myself. Dancing made me feel alive. It was in my bones. I started to laugh to myself as I watched Shivon go for gold with "Mr Random" before I felt a hard tap on my shoulder. Some guy I didn't know was smiling like a Cheshire cat very closely to my face. It was intrusive. He'd also been drinking a bit too much and I could smell it all over his breath. He boldly leaned right into me and slurred, "Youuuu... you wanna dance, babes?"

Before he could get a response, he started singing out of tune and had cheekily put his hand on my waist. He then started rocking side to side (and so *not* in time with the music). *I felt sick*. Now, it has to be said, I am big on personal space and always have been since as long as I can remember, and at this moment it was being invaded on a whole different level. He was sweating and his shirt was saturated. I moved his arm away quicker than you could say "B.O." and told him a very straight and blunt "NO, mate." He backed away, but not without telling me first, how much he couldn't stand girls like me because we all thought we were too nice.

Hmmm, funny that. I think I'm too nice, but YOU were the one who approached ME. Cheek.

I felt another hard tap on my shoulder. I was about to turn around and tell "Mr Sweaty" about himself, but it wasn't him. It was Esther. I was transfixed by her facial expression which had the word *trouble* written all over it. We could see where Shivon was so I knew it wasn't her, and Jenny was on her way back to us from dancing with Gavin. I looked at Esther waiting for her to talk.

"Nats, I can't *believe* him. He takes the mick. I told him you were here but... look; don't go off on one though, girl, he's blatantly drunk."

My heart sank. I took a deep breath before I responded. "Did he come with *her*?" Esther dropped her head and didn't answer. That was all the answer I needed. I looked over to the other side of the bar and I saw Leon with who was obviously his latest "friend". The same one he denied he even knew the week before. He had his arm around her waist and was whispering in her ear seductively. I stood there frozen and mortified, crushed inside, knowing that Leon was up to his usual antics. It was clear what was going on between him and this other female and the thought of it made me want to vomit. He looked up and saw me, nodded as if to say hello, and then went back to making a show of himself. The thoughts that raced through my mind paralysed me.

Oh my dayyyyyyys!! He MUST be drunk. Is he craaaaaaaazy?!! I can't believe this guy. He knew I'd be here tonight and he does THIS! The

amount of years and energy I've spent on this guy and for what? How much more of this am I supposed to take? I can't stand him!

By this time all of my girlies were standing with me and saw what was going on. They were panicking and asking me what I was going to do or if I wanted *them* to do something. I played it cool. I wasn't about to make a fool of myself.

We decided to call it a night. Esther was tired, Shivon's feet were hurting from all of her dance moves, Jenny finally gave Gavin her number, and after what I had just seen I just wanted to go home. The girls made sure I got home okay and spent the whole journey home ranting and raving about how out of order Leon was, how expensive the drinks had got, and we laughed some more at the girl who came in the shoes she couldn't walk in. Esther just wanted to go home and cuddle up with her man. Shivon was high as a kite and had already sent a text to one of her many "links" to meet her at home and keep her company. Jenny was just trying to stay awake and focus on the speed limit so that she wouldn't crash Joel's precious car.

I got home. I was tired, upset and felt spaced out. My phone beeped. I got ready for bed, drank some water, and grabbed for my headscarf before lying down, looking up at the ceiling blank-faced. My phone beeped again. I ignored it. My house was silent but my ears were ringing from all the music in the rave. I couldn't stand it when that happened. There goes the beeping of the phone yet again. I decided to check it. It was a text from Jenny checking if I was okay and another from Esther, and lastly Shivon letting me know what she was about to get up to.

Good for you love.

I turned off the light, closed my eyes and tried to block out the feelings of pain, hurt, and weariness of having to deal with certain aspects of my life. I wanted a change, but I felt trapped. I curled up in the foetal position, and imagined someone giving me a big hug. I usually imagined it was God or just sometimes an imaginary person who would come and take all of my headache away; but to be honest it never felt like God was there or would even waste his time on someone like me.

All of a sudden, I heard a key turning in my front door, and then I heard the door slam shut. I shot up in fear and panic, and turned the bedside lamp on.

Who is in my yard?!

I felt adrenaline rise up in me. I was upset, angry, tipsy, hormonal, and scared but I was ready and willing to hurt someone. Then all of a sudden it hit me. I slowly lay back down, as I realised who had come into my house and I turned the lamp back off. There was only *one* person who knew where I kept my spare key outside. Leon.

He came into my room, turned on my light, and stood at the side of my bed, taking off his shoes. He never said a word. Stupidly, nor did I. I was too emotionally tired. He slumped down onto my bed, and mumbled something about him misplacing the keys to his flat and him going home later that morning.

I couldn't believe his nonchalant, laid back, and totally disrespectful attitude. But I didn't have the energy to challenge him. I went to check that my front door was locked properly, and by the time I came back to see if Leon had anything more to say for himself, he was fast asleep, snoring and sprawled out on my bed with his clothes on.

I had two choices. The first choice was to wake him up and kick him out. After his disgusting behaviour that night, that was the least he deserved. But I knew that if I attempted to do this, I would either be ignored, verbally attacked, or God knows what else. It all depended on what mood Leon was in. As I stood there looking at him I felt disgusted, and I couldn't bear to be anywhere near him. So I soon found myself in tears, feeling very uncomfortable, as I pitifully attempted to make the most of my make shift bed idea on my cold leather sofa.

That was the second choice.

Okay, I know what you're thinking and you're probably right. My name is Natalie, and this book is a collection of different snapshots of my life... my journey. A series of events that contributed to the making of the person I have now become. A reflective account of the times when I thought that my choices and circumstances had the best of me. I spent years believing so much junk about myself, and about life in general, but it was life changing to discover that how my life was, didn't have to stay that way... and it didn't.

SOWING SEEDS

1

It's not the one who plants or the one who waters who is at the centre of this process but God, who makes things grow.

1 Corinthians 3:7 (MSG)

"Lard have mercy! Look how yuh favour Sister Reed! Look how yuh get big an' grow nice."

I loved Sister Stewart but every time I bumped into her in Tesco, she would always say the same thing. All she could ever talk about was how much I looked like my nan, and every time she did, I would have to react like it was the very first time she said it.

I vividly remember going to church with my nan when I was small. I can also remember the special relationship she had with Sister Stewart and a few of the elder women in the church, who were clearly part of my nan's little posse. Sister Stewart was particularly close with my nan, as they had known each other since they were young women, and she was also like an aunty to my mum. I was also really good friends with Sister Stewart's granddaughter Sarah. We were like twins and were always together. We would go to Sunday school together, we would play and hang around together, and undoubtedly get up to mischief together. We were inseparable on a Sunday. After Nenna died, and once Sarah moved away, we lost contact and didn't see each other again.

Nenna. That's what I called my nan. I loved my Nenna indescribably. She used to call me Natsie and I loved the nickname. Most of my memories of going to church with Nenna are fond as well as hilarious. I remember Nenna and her church sisters jumping up and down in church like they were having a fit sometimes when the music was playing. I used to seriously think something was wrong with them, but they seemed happy enough as they sang, stomped their feet and raised their hands. I could never comprehend where they got the energy from, yet come rain or shine, Nenna would always find the energy to sing her heart away in her strong West Indian accent:

"We shall have a gran' time up in heaven. We shall have a gran' time hup in heaven, have a grand tiiiiime..."

Every Sunday, my job was to carry her tambourine (which she would play enthusiastically and very loudly) to and from church. Then the second we would leave church and get on the bus to travel home, she would sit down and start to puff and pant and make noises highlighting the obvious fact that she was in pain, and I would literally count down in my mind and wait for it. I'd say to myself, "... three... two... one... here she goes" and then cue Nenna with her weekly rant of, "Larrrrd... woy... Jesus. Me cyarn tek de whole heap ah pain dem" as she winced and rubbed her knees. Then the routine would continue with complaints by Nenna, Sister Stewart, and the other church sisters on the bus about their arthritis and diabetes, followed by another song or hymn sung in unison:

"It soon be done, all de troubles an' trials, when I get home on de other siiiiide..."

Sarah and I would laugh so hard that we'd struggle to catch our breath. To make matters worse, we had the pressure of laughing while trying hard to not get seen doing it at the same time. Nenna was cool but she didn't play around when it came to discipline. She was old school. I learned from a very young age that it was best to keep most of my overzealous thoughts and opinions to myself around her. I valued the amount of teeth I had in my mouth, and intended on keeping all of them. Plus, Nenna used to buy the best vanilla ice cream in the world, and she refused to tell me where she brought it from, but it was without a doubt my favourite. If I got on the wrong side of her, I knew they'd be no vanilla ice cream treats, and that simply wasn't an option for me.

Nenna mentioned God in most of her conversations or comments. I would smile and nod in response to her, but I never really understood much of what she would say. She also sang a lot around the house and it was about Jesus each and every time. I didn't know who this Jesus person was at the time, but He sure made her smile and as long as Nenna was smiling it was all good because no moaning had to be endured, and rice and peas and chicken was on the table as soon as we got home from church. It made the constant smell of moth balls, Deep Heat, Bay Rum, Wray and Nephews rum, and God knows what other drinks and ointments in the house, worth inhaling. As long as Nenna was cool everyone else was cool.

My granddad, on the other hand, was quiet. He just used to sit in the same worn down brown leather chair, drink rum, and never spoke much. Whenever Granddad spoke, he always had an answer or solution for something. He never really said much unless it was something worth saying. In fact, I'm sure that both of my grandparents had a remedy for absolutely everything in life. No matter what the problem was, they had a song for everything and some kind of saying for everything, whether it made sense or not.

I loved them and only really grew to appreciate them and their so-called "weird" sayings (which actually turned out to be a fountain of wisdom), when it was too late to tell them thanks; when it was too late to tell them that if I applied a lot of their advice once I was old enough to understand what they meant, maybe I would have escaped a lot of problems and hardship. Granddad died when I was ten. Nenna wasn't quite the same after he died. It was as though she was half alive. Nenna died in her sleep a year and a half later. I miss her a lot.

"So tell me, Natsie, how is Mammy?" My deep thought was interrupted. "Natsie... me seh how is Mammy?"

Sister Stewart was peering hard at me through her glasses waiting for an answer.

Why are your glasses so THICK? It makes your eyes look five times the size.

"Who, Mum? Yeah she's okay you know, Sister Stewart." She stood there looking at me as though she wanted me to expand on my answer - but that wasn't going to happen. My mum didn't like to be discussed, especially with anyone from Nenna's old church. Although Sister Stewart was the exception, she didn't want to risk any of her business getting back to anyone she had a problem with. I'd asked my mum about what her problem was with Nenna's church a few times in the past but she didn't like to talk about it much. All I'd managed to piece together was that Mum used to love singing, and this had begun when she attended church with Nenna as a child. I knew this firstly, because Nenna told me. Secondly, I'd seen quite a few old pictures hung up in Nenna's house and figured that Mum must have been quite good at it. There were pictures of her singing in the choir at church when she was little and pictures of her with medals at competitions she'd won. Then Mum got pregnant with me at seventeen. As I grew up, the only related pictures I accidently stumbled across at home were of Mum looking somewhat older and singing again, but this time in clubs and bars. When it came to singing, Mum reminded me a lot of Nenna. She sang around the house just like her. She hummed away just like her. But she definitely wasn't singing about Jesus.

Soon enough, the singing became less frequent as I got older, and I never got the chance to see the same twinkle in her eye that she had in those photos of when she was singing away at competitions or in the choir all those years ago. I never really knew a lot about Mum and Nenna's relationship, and doubt I'll ever really find out the real depths and dynamics of it, but I do know that it was strained.

"How's Sarah, Sister Stewart?" I asked. "I haven't seen her in years."

Sister Stewart went on to tell me how well Sarah was doing and took me on a trip along memory lane where she didn't hesitate to remind me of all the mischief we both used to get up to. She chuckled mischievously as she shared her memories on how our tiresome behaviour and love for dancing would wear her out. That was the main reason why Sarah and I became friends in the first place – our love for dancing. Once we realised that we shared the same passion, there was no stopping us. Everything was about dancing and making up new dance moves and routines that we could show other people. We were always trying to out do each other. As Sister Stewart kept talking, all the memories came flooding back. I remember thinking at the time that it would be really nice to catch up with

Sarah and reminisce about back in the day. Sister Stewart gave me Sarah's number and then swiftly turned the conversation back to the topic of my mum.

"When you speak wid yu' mammy, tell har fe come visit de church, yu' hear, darling?"

Sister Stewart had a big smile on her face. She was a cute old woman even though she had a little moustache thing going on, but it was them *glasses*. I just couldn't get over them horrible, thick, hideous glasses.

"Yeah I will," I replied quickly.

Yeah right, that's a blatant lie.

I knew it was for the best to leave well alone. Although Mum was cool with Sister Stewart, it wasn't worth the millions of questions she would ask me about the whole conversation, and besides, I needed to borrow her deep fat fryer that evening, so the plan was to keep her in a good mood - not reflecting on negative aspects of her past... whatever they were. I felt like frying some chicken that day. I hadn't cooked fried chicken in ages, and I'd made a promise to Daniel to make him his favourite.

My Dandans. I loved him so much. He always managed to temporarily get my mind off of Leon, life, and every other source of stress. He just had a knack for it. I quickly gave Sister Stewart big hug and kiss goodbye, nodded and smiled and nodded some more, and pretended to listen to her as she continued to babble on about something to do with getting home to watch some Bruce Forsyth programme. I was in a hurry, had heard enough, and didn't want to strain my eyes anymore looking at her thick glasses. I paid for my food, and then rushed back down to the frozen section as I had forgotten my vanilla ice cream (which, I must add, was *nothing* like the one Nenna used to buy). After that, I left Tesco in record time so I could go and spend some time with my Dandans. I missed him.

Daniel, by the way, was my six year old son with Leon.

When The Load Gets Heavy   2

Can any one of you by worrying
add a single hour to your life?

Matthew 6:27 (NIV)

I have told you these things, so that in Me you may have
[perfect] peace and confidence. In the world you have tribula-
tion and trials and distress and frustration; but be of good cheer
[take courage; be confident, certain, undaunted]! For I have
overcome the world. [I have deprived it of power to harm you
and have conquered it for you.]

John 16:33 (AMP)

"I'm sorry, I'm going to have to get started otherwise we will run into another parent's appointment time."

I smiled awkwardly and nodded, but I was boiling and bubbling up with anger inside. This was the second time Leon had done this foolishness. It was Daniel's parents evening and I was annoyed because I rearranged the appointment with the teacher *just* because Leon said he'd be there, and in typical Leon style - he didn't turn up. I was so embarrassed. I patiently sat there with Mr Harvey for the next fifteen minutes listening to him tell me how much potential Daniel had. I didn't want to hear anything about potential. I wanted my son to be thriving *now*, like how he had been when he first started the school. Deep down, I knew he wasn't doing his best because things were bothering him, and I couldn't help but think that it had something to do with life for him at home.

"He's a very clever boy, but I have noticed a decline in the standard of his work over this last term. His behaviour has also been quite disruptive which is very unlike him."

Mr Harvey paused and looked at me with a strange glare in his eye, as if he was trying to read me. I really didn't know what he expected me to say. He took another sip of his coffee and exhaled quite heavily through his nose.

Man, I really wish you wouldn't do that, Mr Harvey.

The smell of coffee on his breath was over-powering and the amount of hair he had sprouting out of his nostrils was not a good look. "I was wondering if everything is all right at home," he finally said. Mr Harvey sat back in his chair waiting for a response to his statement (well I took it as a statement, because if it was a question he should've just come straight out and asked me if something was going on. As far as I was concerned, he could go ahead and wonder).

I looked down at my son, who was looking up at me with an anxious look on his face. Daniel dropped his head and started fiddling with his new aeroplane toy I'd bought him the day before. I looked back at Mr Harvey. My face was blank. I really didn't know what to say. What exactly was I supposed to say? *"Actually, Mr Harvey, my son's dad is a wotless individual who says things he doesn't mean and makes promises just to break them, and hardly spends any quality time with Daniel; yet it's muggings here who has to answer all of Daniel's questions, pick up the pieces, and deal with his behaviour when his fool of a dad is running around on road doing God knows what"*. I couldn't say that could I? Would Mr Harvey even know what "wotless" meant? Instead, I put on my fake "everything is under control" smile, and reassured Mr Harvey that all was well and that I would be speaking to Daniel about his school work and behaviour as a matter of urgency.

Mr Harvey continued to show me Daniel's work, but I wasn't sure whether it was a good idea or not. It wasn't as if he was telling me something that I didn't know. I didn't *need* anyone to tell me that my son's behaviour was changing and that it was affecting his school work. I knew it already. I guess I just hoped that my suspicions wouldn't have been con-firmed at the parents evening, and that by some miraculous way, he would be doing as well as he was before. Wishful thinking.

My time was up, so I shook Mr Harvey's sweaty hand, and got up to leave with Daniel. I couldn't wait to get out of there. I was annoyed. I real-ly wanted to call Leon and tell him about himself, but I knew that if I did, the conversation would've been entirely unproductive and all of my emo-tions and frustration towards him in general would have poured out, because at that moment I felt a mixture of disappointment, hurt, and an-ger. I did however, begin to dial his number, but as soon as I pressed the call button I felt Daniel pulling on my coat impatiently. I didn't want Dan-iel to be in ear shot of my conversation so I cut the call off before it could connect. *God knows*. If I had managed to get in contact with Leon at that moment I would've lost my cool and ended up apologising to my son af-terwards. I'd then spend the rest of the day at home feeling guilty for exposing him to that rubbish. That would then lead to me taking out the brandy, and then calling up a mate of mine who lived up the road (who we called Shanks), to ask him to bring me a spliff. Then I'd smoke and drink my life away once Daniel had gone to bed followed by going into "I'm a bad mum" mode, as I'd sit there in self-pity, knowing that I'd let us both down. I couldn't be dealing with that, so I figured that it was best to wait until later to make the call. I considered calling Jenny to moan to her in-stead, but before I could make my mind up, Daniel started to ask questions.

"Muuuum... why didn't Dad come to see my teeacherrrrr?" Daniel was sulking and whining.

"Daddy's a bit busy, Dandans" I said. Then Daniel pulled that face that used to weaken me and make me give in. His bottom lip would slightly drop and his eyes would begin to look glassy as though he was about to cry.

"I tell you what, let's go to McDonald's, Son." I hoped that would do the trick for the time being, and it did. Daniel ran off excitedly. "Fanks, Mum!" he shouted.

On the way to McDonald's, he decided to step up onto a low brick wall and walk along it as quick as he could, trying to balance. Then he jumped off and got back on again. This was a usual thing for Daniel. He was so active. In addition to this, he was swinging his school bag as though he was purposely trying to dislocate his own shoulder, then he changed his game plan and began to attempt to walk along the wall again - but *backwards* this time.

"Dandans, don't do that! Just be careful... in fact come down off of there please." I looked at my son and wondered where he got all of his energy from. Just *watching* him made me tired.

"I'll come down, but only if I'm allowed to get a chicken sandwich, Mum."

I looked at Daniel like he'd lost his mind. Then I smiled inside. He was so cheeky and overconfident. He reminded me so much of his dad.

By the time we got to McDonald's I was exhausted. I'd had a long day. I was working in retail at the time, and was waiting until a few months had passed so that I could enrol at college to begin a course. I despised my job, but I did have a laugh with the other staff there. The main reason why I took the job was because I had a lot of choice with my hours, which conveniently worked around Daniel and his school times. That particular week, and at Leon's request, I'd swapped my shift with my colleague Raj, and the fact that Leon didn't even have the decency to turn up angered me. I wasn't impressed.

I was hungry when I initially arrived at the parents evening, but by the time we got to McDonald's, I was so upset that I didn't feel like eating. My mind kept going over different things. Mr Harvey's words... Leon not turning up... Daniel's questions. Then on top of it I had to deal with the stares and glares of other parents as I was leaving. There were a significant number of parents in the school hall and all that stood out to me was one thing - fathers were alongside the mothers. I didn't care if they were actually couples, if they were happily married, or if they had a messed up relationship; all I cared about at that second was that *my* son's dad wasn't there. I could feel people's eyes on us as we were leaving. My mind began working overtime imagining what they were probably thinking:

Awwwww, look at her... another single mother.

Of course I didn't know what they were *actually* thinking. Maybe I was just being paranoid. I also didn't know if I could actually feel their stares and glares piercing into my back when I was leaving, or if I was just hot because the air con hadn't been turned on. All I knew was that I was tired of having to deal with constant negativity, and I made a decision that I really needed to evaluate how I was going to deal with the effect Leon was having on our son.

I took a bite of one of Daniel's chicken nuggets and decided to get something to eat after all. I had no intention of cooking when I got home, so I bought a milkshake and a Big Mac burger. When I sat down to eat it, I decided that I meant business. I intended on fully devouring that burger. The mood I was in, that Big Mac didn't know what it was in for. I opened the box and picked it up to take a bite whilst contemplating what my next move with Leon would be at the same time. I took a huge bite of the burger and looked down. At least a quarter of the burger had fallen out. Lettuce, gherkins, and sauce smothered my jeans as well as the table, and one of the flimsy burgers were leaning out of the side of the bun, about to fall out.

"Cha man!" I blurted out in frustration.

The fact that Daniel was laughing his head off didn't help the situation either. I also knew that this gave him even more satisfaction because I didn't buy him the chicken sandwich that he'd asked for. I was disgruntled, but I tried not to laugh at the same time because Daniel's cackle of a laugh was very contagious. I also didn't want to laugh because I was frustrated. Leon annoyed me, Mr Harvey's nostrils irritated me, being surrounded by two parent families upset me, and McDonald's annoyed me too, for having them lying adverts that showed the Big Mac looking very different to how my one looked right then. I felt mad at *everyone* and *everything*, but as I'd spent good money for the burger, I made an attempt to shove it back together and devour it anyway, regardless of what it looked like. Different things were going through my mind...

Natalie, this is disgusting. You cannot be serious. Look at the state of the burger.

But then my opposing thought stepped in and I preferred that thought instead:

Cha, I don't business - I spent my money and I don't intend on wasting it.

Considering that I was quite annoyed, I have to admit that I finished that burger quite fast.

I smelt a strong, lingering, and breath taking scent of aftershave. I recognised the scent because I didn't smell it too often. Before I had a chance to put a face to the scent, I looked up and saw "that guy". That nice suit wearing, chiselled-faced looking guy that worked in the bank over the road. He'd served me from time to time, and *every time* I went in there, I made sure that I looked on point. He smiled at me as he walked passed.

"You alright?" he asked, followed by a smile. I smiled back at him and tried to act cool, then watched him as he walked out the door with his food. It was as though everything was happening in slow motion as I sat there totally captivated and gleeful.

Oh my days! I wasn't alright before but I sure am now! Eeeeesh!!

My mind wandered off into a daydream whilst sipping on my milkshake.

"My aeroplane!!! Mum, I left my aeroplane at school."

You have just got to be kidding me. This is all I need.

"Daniel, what is the *matter* with you?! I only bought that for you yesterday, do you think I've got money out here to be wasting?!" I yelled.

Couldn't I even have a daydream in peace? I really didn't have the energy to go all the way back to the school but I felt so bad for Daniel, especially with his dad not turning up, and I didn't want him to be upset any further. Daniel began to cry as if his whole world was falling apart. I knew that parents evening was still going on so I'd probably be able to get the aeroplane back if someone hadn't gone with it. By the time we got back to the school, I had a stitch because of the rushing, Daniel wanted to go wee, and I just seriously wanted to go home and get under the duvet and feel sorry for myself. As I rushed towards the school hall, I heard one of the receptionists shout my name out. I turned around to answer and I saw Cathy with a cheeky smile on her face, waving Daniel's aeroplane in her hand.

"A certain little boy wouldn't happen to be looking for *this* by any chance would he?"

Daniel raced up to her and snatched his aeroplane. I didn't know who was more thankful, Daniel or me.

"Aww thanks Cathy, you've saved me from a lot of ear ache tonight," I said dryly.

"No problem. One of the teachers gave it in," she said. "Are you okay? You look like how I feel."

"Don't even get me started."

Cathy smiled again.

On leaving the school, I was taking pigeon steps home. My legs felt like lead and I was tired. I heard the sound of a car horn, followed by someone shouting my name. It was Esther and Mark. I walked up to the car and Daniel ran ahead of me to say hello to Justin, Esther's son.

"Wassup, girl! Did you just have your appointment? Where's Leon at?" Esther asked.

By the look on my face as a response to her question, Esther knew that her questioning should stop right there. I greeted Mark and then pulled a silly face at Justin, who was at the back of the car. Justin and Daniel went to the same school, and although they weren't in the same class they were very close.

"You got your appointment now, Ess?"

"Yeah, girl," Esther said excitedly. Unfortunately, I wasn't sharing the same excitement.

"Listen, I'm proper tired and I need to get Dandans home so bell me later."

"Alright, Nats. Oh, Natalie, look…"

Esther was wiping the side of her face, but looking at mine. I didn't understand what she was doing at first, but then I realised that she was trying to tell me that I had something at the side of my face that needed to be wiped away. I looked into the side mirror of the car to see what it was, and I saw a large amount of dried tomato ketchup smothered on the side of my face. I wasn't amused. Everyone was silent at first, then the silence was followed by a crescendo of laughter, but I however, didn't share the joke.

Couldn't Cathy have told me? Couldn't Daniel have said? Cha man!

When I considered the fact that "that guy" in McDonald's was probably smiling hard because of the ketchup on my face rather than his joy to see me, I wanted the floor to swallow me up. I quickly said my goodbyes and Esther and Mark parked up the car and went into the school with Justin. I watched them walking in. I smiled... I sighed.

By the time I got home and put Daniel to bed, I was totally exhausted. I sat down and began flicking through the television channels. I watched a programme for a while, but if you asked me what I was watching, I wouldn't be able to tell you. I felt a tear roll down my face, and I was staring into space. It was almost as if I didn't realise that I was crying. I was spaced out. I was thinking about the day. I thought about Leon... about my son's disappointed face... about the teacher's patronising tone... and even that stupid ketchup on my face. I thought about Esther, and how I wished that Daniel had a dad like Mark.

I went to check on Daniel before the weed and brandy began to sink into my system. He was cuddled up with his aeroplane. I picked it up to put it on his bedside table and realised that one of the wings was broken. *Great*. I didn't have the money to simply go out and get him another one so I decided that he would just have to wait until Christmas, and in the meantime I'd have to get him something else.

Christmas. I didn't even want to think about it. Christmas meant family and together they equalled headache. I started thinking about previous Christmases and couldn't figure out if the thought of them was giving me a headache or if the brandy was.

I took another swig of my second glass of brandy, and finished smoking the spliff that I'd got Shanks to drop off to me earlier that evening, and then went into the very same mode that I didn't intend to go into earlier on that day. But I just needed to not think... to not feel... because I knew that the next time I would speak to Leon, there would probably be a whole lot of drama and I knew that I needed all the energy I could muster. Until then, I just wanted to sink into my sofa and switch off. I just wanted to get away. From what? Myself, I guess... oh... and from reminiscing about Christmas.

What's Done In The Dark 3

For everything that is hidden will eventually be brought into the open, and every secret will be brought to light

Mark 4:22 (NLT)

Christmas day at my great aunt's house was always a drama. In fact *every* Christmas was a drama. Another time of year when everyone got together and pretended we were one big happy family. Now don't get me wrong, my family weren't as dysfunctional as some other families I'd encountered, but we never did much throughout the year as a family, so Christmas to me was just a time of year when everything was a bit false and forced.

There is one year in particular that sticks out like a sore thumb in my mind, and this was many years ago when we spent Christmas at my great aunt's house. Aunty Herda was my nan's younger sister (Nenna's younger sister). All of the family would pass through her house during the day at one point or another. The one thing that I appreciated about the day was the abundance of food and drink. In fact, there was probably about enough to feed every household on her street. It was ridiculous, but nothing ever went to waste.

Aunty Herda's house was like an open house most of the time throughout the year, so Christmas day wasn't an exception. This particular year, I was still doing my thing with Leon and Daniel was a baby. Most Christmases, Leon would insist on gate crashing whoever's home I was at, even if it was just for a drink. His attendance usually depended on how well we were getting on at the time, or what our "status" was, because our relationship was frequently on and off.

Spending time with my girlies was a standard procedure, but with Es-

WHAT'S DONE IN THE DARK

ther being the exception. Every year, she spent the entire day with her parents. No visitors, and no Esther popping out to see her friends. Her family had strict views on Christmas celebrations and spending time together privately as a family.

Seeing Shivon at some point throughout the day was a yearly priority for me. Unfortunately, she didn't have much family, and was estranged from most of them. For most years, she would spend Christmas with her foster parents, but once she moved out, she'd spend the day at her own flat or someone else's home. She wasn't picky, but I could be sure that no matter what she was doing, even if we both knew that we would see each other later on in the day, Shivon would still pop her head in for an alcohol beverage - *regardless* of where I was. Year after year, from childhood to adulthood, she'd insist that she wasn't bothered about the whole "Christmas thing", but all of us knew it was a front, so we unceasingly made the effort to spend time with her at that particular time of year. As for Jenny (who was practically like family), she would find herself *wherever* I found myself, or I would visit her, Joel, and the rest of her family. Whatever the arrangement, we would *always* see each other. That was the usual.

This particular year was the same old thing apart from the fact that *this* year, I found out some very interesting information that finally helped me put a few pieces of the puzzle together regarding my mum and my aunt's relationship.

I'd spent the morning at the hostel I was living in at the time with Daniel. Leon came to pick us up late that morning, but wanted to spend the majority of the day at his dad's house with Daniel. I didn't fancy going with him to endure his loud-mouthed cousins and equally annoying family members, plus I had to help out at Aunty Herda's with food preparation. I arrived in the afternoon and made sure that I made my usual trip to the same old corner shop that was always open, to purchase some Paracetamol. I always made sure I had some with me, because even the deaf would be able to hear the bass line of the music coming from the house. Notting Hill Carnival couldn't compete with Aunty Herda's reggae, revival and soca music pumping out of her speakers. I felt sorry for the neighbours.

Mum was in the kitchen doing a million and one things as usual. I think she loved being busy so that she didn't really have to mingle too much with other people. She was perfectly happy doing her domestic thing, while singing away to classic Gregory Isaacs and Dennis Brown songs. She seemed to have everything under control with about five pots on the go and masses of food everywhere else in the kitchen. I could see that she hadn't started preparing the macaroni cheese, so I grated the cheese for her. Shortly afterwards, I heard someone stomp into the kitchen, but I didn't turn around to see who it was.

"Yuh wash yu han', gyal?"

I didn't even have to turn around. I'd recognise his voice anywhere. It was Uncle Dennis. His accent was strong, and his voice was deep. He had a big smile on his face, as usual, and he came straight over to me and gave me a big hug. I could just about breathe, he was hugging me so hard. I embraced him back, and although I loved my uncle, I felt awkward so I cut the hug short. Like I've said before – I'm big on personal space. Uncle Dennis was really coarse and abrupt in his manner, so if you didn't know him personally, you could take him the wrong way. I was used to how he was, and he and I were cool. No matter what time of year it was, he would be prancing around the house wearing a string vest stretched over his large pot belly. He would religiously have a can of drink in his hand, and I'd lost count of the amount of gold teeth he had in his mouth. His hairline had gone beyond receding, but although this man was in his sixties, he thought he was the hottest thing ever to walk the streets of London. He was Aunty Herda's "partner". Looking back on it, I really have to laugh at my naivety. You see, I grew up thinking that they were married because they had been together longer than the years I'd been alive, but my mum told me around that time that they wasn't married, and never had been married... but Uncle Dennis *was* married; and had been for twenty-six years. *You* do the math.

"Yes, Uncle, my hands are clean."

He stood there for about two minutes smiling and checking them thoroughly.

"Yes, mek sure, becar mi nuh able fe' mi belly fe' start hurt at aaall, at aaall, at aaall, at aaaaaaalll sah." I had to laugh. I've repeatedly found the interesting choice of expressions used by the older generation of my family, quite comical. Like Uncle Dennis just then. The way he repeats or stretches out a word to really express or emphasise it.

How is stretching out the word or repeating it so much going to make any kind of difference to what you're saying, Uncle D?

Then he did it again, complaining about the heat in the kitchen. "Mi seh mi hot, mi hot, mi hot sah! It hot een ya eee?" I smiled and kept my thoughts to myself.

Yes, Uncle Dennis, it's hot. You only had to say it once.

Mum was still making herself busy in the kitchen, and had gone from singing to swaying from side to side to some soca music. "Natalie, how did the vests and stuff I bought for Dandans fit him? And what time is he coming with that wotless man of yours?"

I loved my mum, I really did, but sometimes she didn't have to go there. I knew Leon had his ways, but her constant reminders wasn't needed.

"They fit him, Mum, and he'll be here later. Leon's gonna call me," I mumbled unenthusiastically. I thought that my tone would be enough to stop her from going on, but it wasn't.

"I'm telling you, Natalie, big Christmas Eve, and he couldn't even come round here to drop off some drinks. But I bet he'll be here drinking them off later on though innit? Bwoy, Natalie, I dunno where you picked him up from."

I'd already tried to explain to my mum that Leon couldn't help out the previous night to drop anything down to Aunty Herda's house, because he had to do a few things for his dad. It had clearly gone into one ear and out the other, as I found myself spending the next three minutes reminding her of the situation. She just looked at me, then looked away and said "Hmm" sharper than the knife she was devouring some onions with. I don't even know if she actually *said* "Hmm" because it was more like a grunt. To get the focus off of me, I changed the subject and started talking to her about the present I'd given her. Her face lit up like a child in a toy store when she started telling me what she planned to do with the money I'd given her towards her new exercise bike.

"Watch me, Natsie, I'm gonna be looking well and truly trim in a few months."

By this time, Mum had forgotten about the food preparation and was now elegantly stroking her waist and hips, showing where she wanted to lose weight. She strolled up and down the kitchen like she was on a catwalk, dressed to impress with her house shoes and apron on.

"Plus, this belly is well and truly bang and it's gotta go!"

Without hesitation, we burst into fits of laughter. It'd been a good few weeks since I'd last seen my mum *smile*, let alone laugh. Maybe it was because it was Christmas. Maybe it was because she was going to get her new exercise bike. I didn't care; the main thing was that she was laughing, and it was nice to witness.

We spent the rest of the afternoon eating and drinking, and laughing and dancing while friends and family passed through Aunty Herda's house. Cousin Pearl came to the house, drunk as a skunk as per usual. She was in her late fifties at the time. All of her children were grown, but come rain or shine you could rely on her to be wearing clothes that her granddaughters wouldn't even think about wearing. She was embarrassing, but she made me laugh because she was actually convinced that she looked really good, even when she wasn't drunk. I'd tried to tell her many times before (and in the nicest possible way) that Lycra wasn't for everyone, and that her curly perm hairdo really didn't need so much grease, but since the time she accused me of being jealous of her, I quit trying to talk to her.

In the evening, Desireé came round just after dinner, with her new fiancé. She was my aunt. My mum's sister. I didn't call her Aunty because she told me when I was small to call her by her name since "Aunty" made her feel old. Whenever she was around, the atmosphere changed. People started clearing their throats and avoiding eye contact with her, or finding different topics of conversation hoping that Desireé wouldn't join in. Let's just say, just like Cousin Pearl, she was another on a long list of what I like to call the T.F.M list – Tolerated Family Members list. Most of the tension would usually be between Mum and Desireé. I never understood why, but got used to it and accepted it as the norm since I was small. Nenna and Aunty Herda had continuously tried to encourage a close relationship between them, but it just didn't happen. I'd heard that even Sister Stewart made a few attempts in their younger years. The thing with them was that, they wouldn't really argue as such, but there was no display of affection, and every conversation shared would always consist of sarcasm and patronising or harsh tones. Desireé was cool, but since studying law (and taking up the habit of shacking up with men who were financially well off, to fund the up keep of her image and materialistic lifestyle), she seemed to habitually flaunt it in front of the family. She thought she was a cut above us all, but everyone could see behind all that L'Oreal. We all knew her game, and this particular Christmas we didn't expect anything different.

Her new fiancé, Hugh, was a tall white man who smelled good, dressed well, and looked a good few years her senior. He had a weird haircut and constantly had this bizarre facial expression which I didn't like. They did *not* look good together, but then again, that was never a problem for Desireé. He was divorced, owned several houses, and apparently lived somewhere near Kensington at the time. That was a good enough CV for my aunt. He looked like a total misfit being in the house, but my family was always welcoming. Uncle Dennis wasted no time in taking Hugh outside to show him the art of how the family played dominoes. Hugh looked a little taken aback at the way all the men were slamming the dominoes down on the make-shift table in the garden, but he tried to keep a straight face. I thought it was hilarious.

My mum offered Hugh a plate of food, which he welcomed gladly. Everyone else was scattered in and around the house, talking, laughing, eating, and drinking. I spent a little while in the garden chilling and talking to Shivon. Jenny had already come and gone. Shivon was lecturing me about studying dance and taking my ability to dance seriously, but I didn't want to think about anything like that at the time. After she dropped the topic, we were laughing at some of my family members dance moves, when we were interrupted by some commotion we heard coming from inside the house. I thought it was my imagination at first, then I thought maybe the reggae music was too loud, but then I heard Desireé shouting. I rushed inside and Shivon followed me, chicken drumstick in one hand, rum and coke in the other. Mum and Desireé were arguing.

"If I wanted him to have food I would have given him some myself!! We're particular about what we eat. No one asked you to make yourself useful did they? Now look at the state of him!"

Desireé was upset with Mum and had begun to shout at her because she'd put just a little bit too much hot pepper sauce on Hugh's food. This had resulted in him choking his head off accompanied by his face taking on the same shade as a beetroot.

"Listen Desireé, don't start me off today you hear mi! I asked the man if he wanted the sauce and he said yes. It's not *my* fault de man couldn't handle it," Mum barked. I knew Mum was upset because that's when the West Indian accent would become noticeably stronger in her speech.

Desireé was exasperated. She continued shouting at Mum.

"Anyone with common sense would have seen that was too much sauce, Sandra, but hey... sense is one thing you don't seem to have, but as for the *common* part..."

At that point Mum spun around so fast, I thought she was going to fall over. The look she had on her face was one I've never seen before. Her eyes were bulging out of her head.

"Desireé, let me tell you something one time and one time only..."

Gradually, some of the family had gathered into the kitchen. Aunty Herda walked over to Mum and held her arm tightly, almost like she anticipated her lashing out. She looked angrily at Desireé and then cautiously back at Mum before speaking.

"Come on now, unu stop de foolishness now man, stop!" I could hear the panic and anxiousness in Aunty Herda's voice. "If unu madda was still alive, she wouldn't stand fe it, so unu stop it!"

There was something in my mum's eyes that told me that whatever Aunty Herda was saying *wasn't* registering.

"Desireé…" Mum glared at her and continued calmly and coldly, "You are a nasty, slack, woman an' yuh mek me *sick*. This same food your precious Hugh is eating was the same food you grew up on but all of a sudden you tink yuh too good fe everybody."

Desireé angrily attempted to respond. "Who the -"

"Shut your mouth, I'm NOT FINISHED!!" Mum screamed, cutting her off.

Desiree was silent. Mum was so mad she dropped the glass she was drying. She bent down to pick up the broken glass, took a deep breath and looked Desireé straight in the eye.

"You might think I'm common because I don't have the same job as you, because I don't mingle with the same people as you do and pretend to be someone I'm not, but I tell you something; anyone can bleach their skin, wear a bruk' down weave, and sleep their way to the top with any and everybody; sit down in a country club and nyam cucumber sandwiches, then sneak off to Kentucky Fried Chicken when they leave like *you* do, but I choose *not* to live my life like that, so check yourself! And I tell you another thing, you might think you're special, but remember that while yu' ah run roun' tryna keep up with the Joneses, I have something that you will *never* have… KIDS! So just remember dat!"

Desiree smiled and started laughing – it was a smug and sinister laugh. Initially, I didn't understand her response, but I became even more bewildered and dumbfounded after her next statement.

"*Kids*?" she spewed. "You mean *kid*. Your little boy's DEAD remember Sandra?"

"Lard, have mercy!" Uncle Dennis belted out in shock.

Mum, still having the broken glass in her hand, went into a complete blind rage and lunged at Desireé, but Uncle Dennis and a few others rushed to stop her. Profanity shot out of my mum's mouth, and tears of anger streamed down her face as she screamed at the top of her voice threatening to commit murder. I was stunned, shocked, and totally confused. Desireé rushed out of the house with Hugh hurrying along behind her. Mum had totally lost control. I'd *never* seen her like that before, and what was Desireé talking about? I didn't have a *brother*? Did I? I was baffled. And what was Mum talking about? Desireé had always said she didn't have children because she didn't *want* any.

There was a mad frenzy in the kitchen for the next five minutes or so. Mum was fighting with all her might to get to free from my uncles, Aunty Herda was crying, and people were just faffing around not knowing what to do. Shortly afterwards, things calmed down, and Mum was puffing and panting trying to catch her breath. For a few seconds (which felt like an eternity) there was a wave of awkward silence while the music was still playing in the background. No one really knowing what to say. Mum started clearing up plates and banging them down. Aunty Herda started holding her head and shaking it, getting upset, and calling on the Lord. She went after Desireé and was outside for a short while, then came back inside ranting and raving about the argument. Mum was silent. She was so angry that she was shaking, but she continued drying plates, wiping the kitchen sides, and banging cupboards. Aunty Herda continued walking around the house displaying her disturbing combination of cursing, crying, and asking God why this had to happen, whilst Uncle Dennis tried to calm her down. Mum just ignored her and everyone stayed out of Mum's way... including me.

Shivon hadn't moved from where she was standing. The chicken drumstick was still in her hand. The cup with rum and coke in her other hand was now finished and her mouth was wide open in complete shock.

"Rarrr, Nats man, I've never heard your mum go on like dat before man."

"Shiv, not *now*... you know what, I wanna go and get Dandans. Drop me to Leon's."

I got my stuff together, packed up some food for the next day, said my goodbyes to everyone, but was wary of my mum, so I left her until last. I wasn't sure what to say. I didn't know what to think.

"Mum, I'm gonna go and get Dandans, but I'll call you tomorrow."

"Hmm. Okay, Natalie," she grunted. She didn't even turn around to look at me. Man, I just hated those moments. My mum wasn't very affectionate so I didn't want to hug her in case she pushed me away. At the same time, I really wanted to hug her and felt guilty at the same time because I had questions to ask. I didn't want to ask if she was okay because that was obvious, I knew that she wasn't. I figured that it was best to just leave her. It was horrible and awkward.

Shivon dropped me to Leon's. It was silent in the car, and then Shivon broke the silence. I knew she couldn't help herself and had waited to see how long it was going to take her before she started commenting.

"Nats, I didn't know you had a br-" Shivon looked at my face, and didn't bother to finish what she was saying.

I thanked God that Leon was just getting ready to leave when I arrived because I was not in the mood for his family; I just wanted to go home. I remember telling Leon what happened and what my mum had said to Desireé, but I left out the not having kids part, and my mum's dead son part. I needed time to let that settle in my mind.

It would take a few months of indirect questioning of family members and overhearing people's conversations, to help me put some of the pieces together. Apparently, some time after my mum had me she gave birth to a little boy, but he died in hospital before Mum could take him home. I don't know what exactly happened to Mum when she was pregnant, but my dad apparently had something to do with it, which led to complications regarding the baby's death. I had no idea. I was too young to remember Mum being pregnant. As for Desireé, due to some complications with her health, she couldn't have children. She had found this out around the time Mum had given birth to me. Apparently, this particular issue (as well as other things) caused major sibling rivalry between Mum and my aunt. After that Christmas, I don't remember Mum even mentioning Desireé's name again. I really wanted to talk to her about what I'd heard but was too scared to even ask. I hadn't always understood Mum's ways, or why she would do and say certain things, but I always knew that she was strong. She just held it together. If there was one thing I knew to be true, it was definitely that. My mum's heart was a deep ocean of pain, strength, and secrets. It was only as I continued to get older and experience life that I really began to appreciate and understand that *this* truth would be the same for so many other women... myself included.

SEE AND BE BLIND 4

Hear now this, O foolish people without understanding or heart, who have eyes and see not, who have ears and hear not.

Jeremiah 5:21 (AMP)

"The mobile number you have called is currently unavailable. Please check the number and redial."

This is one thing I can't stand about you, Leon. Whenever you need to be contacted, I can't get you. I told you to be ready for a certain time to pick me up from Tesco, and now you're unavailable. It's cold, I'm sitting at the bus stop with shopping bags, and I really just don't have the time for this.

I tried to call him again several times, and every time I called, I got the same result. The longer I sat there watching people leave Tesco and wait no longer than 10 minutes for their bus or cab, the more frustrated I became. I remember seeing a girl around the same age as myself at the time, getting picked up by someone who appeared to be her boyfriend. He also looked a lot like Leon. He got out of the car and put her heavy shopping bags into the boot of his car. I smiled a little, as I saw the anxiety on her face being replaced by a smile of total relief and thankfulness. I sat at the bus stop and began to reminisce as I watched them.

When I first met Leon things were similar to what I had just witnessed. He was always picking me up earlier than the time we'd agreed, being thoughtful, and doing all the things that I thought at the time would make any young woman smile. Of course, it didn't last. I was young and naive enough to think it would. Age and experience have allowed me to see it for exactly what it was – the honeymoon period and unrealistic expectations coupled with the fact that I was in a relationship that I had *no* business being in.

The very first time I became acquainted with Leon was on the night of a mutual friend's birthday drink up. It was our friend Steven's seventeenth birthday and loads of people I knew were there. There was Steven and his brother, Casper, James, and loud mouthed Decks (who Shivon was messing around with at the time). Soldier, Michael, and Blacks were there as well as me and the girlies and lots of other people from all over the area. The atmosphere and behaviour was the same juvenile concoction of flirting, getting drunk, number exchanging, fighting, dancing, smoking, and the constant use of whatever the up to date slang was for that time. In hindsight, I can see that we were all trying to live grown up lives, but really, we were all just young people trying to find ourselves. Everyone had the talk and tried to walk the walk, but none of us really knew who we were.

Once a few hours of everyone joking around and trying to talk over the loud music had passed, I went outside for a bit of fresh air with Jenny.

"Oi, Nats, did you see Decks tryna go on like he was hot when he walked in?" We both laughed until our bellies hurt, as Jenny attempted to impersonate him.

"I hear you, Jen," I said, trying to catch my breath from laughing so hard. "And the thing is, he walked up in the place like he's so hot and he didn't even bother to get a trim! Did you see his hair?!"

Jenny and I were in stitches by then. Esther came outside to join us and she was also trying to get away from some guy who had been bothering her all night. We took one look at her face and unfortunately for her, she became the next joke for us both. Esther didn't find it funny of course, but even *she* had to join in the laughter once we mimicked how her face was set when she initially came outside.

"Narr man, you lot take the mick, it's not even funny," Esther said, trying to keep a straight face. "My dad doesn't even know I'm here, and I have to be dealing with this bug-a-boo guy on top of it! Anyway, forget you lot. Where's Shiv?"

Esther was like the mum of the group, always making sure everyone was okay.

"Where do you think?" Jenny and I sarcastically said in unison. That was a stupid question and Esther knew it was. Wherever the guys were, *that's* where Shivon could be found. Shortly afterwards, the DJ changed up the music and put on one of our favourite slow jams.

"Tuuuuuuune!!" Esther and Jenny screamed, hobbling back into the house in the new shoes that were squeezing their toes. I decided to stay outside for a bit longer. Inside was way too stuffy for me and the cool breeze blowing outside felt nice on my face. I lit a cigarette, inhaled deeply, and then slowly blew out the smoke while distinctly twisting my mouth to one side at the same time. I wasn't sure why I twisted my mouth in that way, and began to wonder about it. It's not like anyone else was outside apart from me, so the smoke wasn't bothering anyone, and I was used to having smoke in my face on a regular basis. I guess it was just habit. As I sat on the wall still pondering on my smoking habits, I heard a voice I didn't recognise.

"So what, you're not coming inside? I know you must be cold out here."

I turned around and I saw a tall guy smiling so hard and intensely, I thought he might run the risk of giving himself a jaw ache. His teeth were *shockingly* white, and his smile was captivating. He was also dressed very much to my taste in those days. I looked straight down to check out his footwear, because if his trainers were mashed up and beat down I would've found it to be a huge turn off. He didn't disappoint. His trainers were fresh and the bottom of his jeans dropped nicely on top of them. His top and his jacket fit him well, and he had a fresh haircut too. Before I had the chance to respond to him, he walked over to me with a little spring and bounce in his step and introduced himself as, Leon.

I introduced myself as "Jenny's friend", and when I did, his facial expression was an unimpressed one. I decided to tell him that because I'd briefly seen him talking to Joel and I knew that he was aware of who Jenny was. Plus, I wasn't totally sure if I was going to give him my number at that point.

"Yeah, I know her, she's Joel's little sister... the girl with the burn on her face right?" he asked.

I nodded, wondering what immature remark he was going to come out with next regarding Jenny's scar. He never mentioned anything else. Instead he said, "I know she's your friend and she's cool an' that but she thinks she's too nice though, and she's not even all dat."

Well, I wasn't having that. Truth be known, Jenny wasn't the most approachable person, and could definitely be a bit of what we then liked to call "stoosh", but she was my friend so I was always going to defend her. After telling him about himself for a few minutes, he shut me up with a bit of sweet talk, telling me how nice my smile was and laying on the charm. It was nothing I hadn't heard before, but there was something about him that I felt drawn to. He was a bit different. Cheeky, or a bit arrogant some might say, but I liked it. *Warning number one.* Sometimes, the things you can like so much about someone in the beginning of a relationship can end up being the very same things that you despise in the end. Of course I didn't realise that then; but sadly, even if I had, I probably wouldn't have cared.

I also liked Leon's ability to finish my sentences when we first got together. I used to think that it expressed how much he understood me. It's quite ironic that by the middle of our relationship, I just wished that he would shut up and let me finish what I was saying.

"So what, Natalie, how you getting home?" Leon asked. "I know you're not driving, 'cause I know your feet must be bunning you in them shoes!"

We laughed. He then went on to admit that he already knew my name, because Steven told him when he asked about me earlier on that evening. We were outside for what seemed like forever, talking, and cracking jokes. He continued to tease me about my hurting feet and I constantly told him to shut up for one reason or another. He was undoubtedly feisty, but he'd been cracking so many jokes and was so annoyingly funny, that I'd already begun to warm to him. He asked me if I was seeing anyone and I wasn't... well not *technically* anyway. Harvey and I had been talking for a few months but nothing ever really came of it.

Leon told me that he'd split up with his ex over a year ago. He also said that he was working part time in JD Sports while he was studying, and expressed how much plans he had for his future. I didn't realise it at the time, but that was the beginning of Leon telling me a lot of things, and sometimes the things just didn't add up. Soon enough, the girlies came to my rescue, but not before Leon and I exchanged numbers. By the look on Jenny's face it was clear that she was not pleased with my present choice of company.

"I just don't like him, girl, he thinks he's too hot, and anyway he's supposed to have some girl up in West London. Chereen... Chantel... Cha-something."

I told her what he'd said about splitting up with his girl over a year ago. "Well if it's not her, there's *bound* to be someone else," she said flatly. I shrugged it off. *Warning number two.*

Everyone was having a good time while Leon and I exchanged glances across Steven's front room. After a while of me trying to look my best and suck in my slightly podgy tummy for the rest of the night, the girls and I decided to leave. Leon and I stole a moment to say our goodbyes in the hallway, ending with his promise to call me. After waiting for Shivon in the car for about half an hour (which was her version of five minutes), we saw Leon and his friends leave the house and walk over to a car.

"Whose BMW is dat? The car is nice man!" Esther asked, wide eyed and intrigued. She was twisting her neck to look at the car so much, I thought her head was going to drop off.

"It's Leon's, innit," Jenny said dryly and completely unimpressed. *Warning number three.* This guy was working in JD Sports part time, and was driving that kind of car? Either he had another source of income, or I needed to change my part time occupation. Although the alarm bells began to ring, I deliberately chose not to pay them much attention at the time. I was too busy trying to come down off of the high of his aftershave scent let alone everything else about him.

After that night Leon called as promised. After many cinema visits, meals, gifts, compliments and gestures, and spending lots of time together we were officially a couple and everyone knew about it.

My mum always used to say to me *"If you can't hear, then you must feel"*. In this instance I should've listened to my instincts, but I chose to ignore them. I had my suspicions about Leon from the very beginning. The more time went on, the clearer things became. There was the way he'd walk out of the room to take his phone calls. The way he would say that he was at a particular place, yet the noises in the surrounding background sounded completely contrary. The times he would come home and take random showers, and just loads of little niggly things. I also was fully aware that he was into all kinds of fraudulent and illegal activities but I didn't ask too many questions because to be honest, I didn't really want to know the details. I was happily living in my own land of denial because of how this guy made me feel. I didn't want to ask any questions that I couldn't handle the answer to. So I didn't ask. When I occasionally chose to confront him on particular things, the way he would react would additionally indicate that there was a reason for me to be suspicious - but fear would kick in. It was fear that if he gave me the bare truth, I would then have to deal with the reality of facing it, and I don't think I wanted to, especially after I found out that I was pregnant. I knew that Leon had a shady and shifty character, but I thought I loved him. The reason why I say *thought* is because, I didn't actually know what real love was until Jesus Christ came into my life.

When Leon told me he loved me, I believed him. I believed him because I *wanted* to believe him – not because I wholeheartedly thought it was true. I thought that his coming home to me every day meant that he loved *me,* regardless of the sad possibility that he may have been coming from somewhere he had no business being. I thought he loved me because he bought me things and helped me pay my bills. Unfortunately, I thought that this was what I was worth. I thought that loved looked this way. He made me feel so high and so low all at the same time, and although I believed I loved him, part of me didn't want to. I wanted better for myself, but wasn't sure if I could actually get it. When I was with Leon, I subconsciously tried to make him fill a massive void in my life. So to my detriment, Leon became my everything.

"The mobile number you have called is currently unavailable. Please check the number and redial." Back at the bus top I was really beginning to get annoyed.

I've been waiting for forty-five minutes for this fool.

I kept looking at the time on my mobile phone hoping that it would suddenly say something different, because I didn't want to accept that I'd been sitting there for so long waiting for Leon, and I really didn't want to think about where I *could* have been at that moment if I had just followed my mind and brought my bus pass with me. Suddenly, I heard a loud car horn. It was him. He jumped out of the car, full of excuses.

"Babe, hear what yeah, there was nuff traffic, and I stopped by Black's yard quickly to drop him something."

I didn't want to hear a word he had to say. "What happened to your phone, Leon?!" I snapped.

"I had bad reception, babes."

We drove in complete silence. Leon's music was on full blast, and he began to chomp hard on the Twix he was eating. *Everything* he was doing was irritating me. He stopped to get some petrol, and asked me if I wanted anything from the shop when he went to pay. I immaturely ignored him. All of a sudden I heard a phone ring, and it certainly wasn't *my* ringtone. I moved around to see where it was coming from, and I realised that Leon had accidentally dropped his mobile phone on the floor of the car. I picked it up and I saw that he had a missed call from "Charles". I put his phone down, but something didn't sit well with me. Number one, that phone number looked too familiar to me, and number two, Charles? No disrespect to anyone called Charles, but if any of Leon's friends at the time had a name like Charles, they would've preferred to be known by a name that was a million miles away from "Charles". The number on his phone was bugging me because I'd seen it before but couldn't remember when. *So I called it*. It rung out and went to voicemail. I listened to the voicemail recording.

"Hi, this is Charlene's phone, leave a message and I'll get back to you." *Charlene.* Okay. Now, either Leon thinks he's smart or "Charles" had a sex change.

FOOLISH OR WISE?

5

Blessed (happy, fortunate, prosperous, and enviable) is the man who walks and lives not in the counsel of the ungodly [following their advice, their plans and purposes]...

Psalm 1:1 (AMP)

'Why do you call Me, 'Lord, Lord,' and do not do what I say?'

Luke 6:46 (NIV)

Has there ever been a period of time in your life when you've felt so emotionally tired, disheartened, and depressed, that a whole week could go by as if it were one day? Well, if you haven't, I must say, it's quite a horrible experience; and if you *have*, well then you'll know exactly what I'm talking about. I experienced this quite frequently during my relationship with Leon. I would spend days at home simply wanting to be on my own and found *everything* a strain to do. It could be the simplest task, yet it would feel as though that *one* task was asking too much of me. I'd have no enthusiasm, and would wander around in auto pilot mode, disengaged from everything and everyone around me. Although I was physically present, the *real* essence of me would seem a million miles away, leaving me feeling totally lost. A numbness would take over, and I would have no care for much of what was going on around me. The metaphor I like to use to best explain this is: The lights are on, but no one's home.

My daily routine would be the same monotonous experience. I'd wake up every morning wondering why I woke up. I would spend hours watching the television, but half of the time, nothing that was happening on the screen was actually registering in my mind. Whenever I hit my lowest points, Daniel would be in his most energetic moods and it was hard to not get irritated. Nevertheless, I would try to look after Daniel to the best of my ability and continue to slap on the smile and try to appear as if all was well; but even the simple things would take up an enormous amount of energy. I could also be doing anything from tying his shoes laces to washing the dishes, yet in a split second I could find myself in a flood of tears for no apparent reason. I didn't like it because I felt out of control, and I didn't want Daniel to pick up on what I was experiencing, or to witness my constant spurts of crying. I tried my best to hide the depth of how I was feeling, but the thing about children is - they're not stupid. They pick up on more than we think.

This is why on those down and out days, I couldn't wait to take him to nursery or school and call in sick at work or college so I could stay at home, be on my own, and take the mask off. I would drop him off and then rush home *praying* that I wouldn't see anyone I knew out of fear of being asked what was wrong.

On some days, I didn't even want to wash my skin. I would just lie in bed or on my sofa with my curtains drawn and mentally switch off. I didn't want to eat either. I was literally anaesthetised, and all of this would usually be the result of some disrespectful action or act of indiscretion carried out by Leon, or our continuous dysfunctional pattern taking its toll on me. If the incident was about cheating (which it usually was) we would argue, and I would cry out of the disappointment of finding out about some female he was either having inappropriate conversations with or sleeping with. Of course he would give it all the big talk and pitifully tell me it was a one off, and make all the excuses he could think of. Sometimes he'd make it seem as if it was all in my imagination. Other times he was unapologetically rude and dismissive. I remember clearly on one occasion he had the bare-faced cheek to boldly say to me *"What do you expect me to do, babes? These gyal dem are all over me, it's hard for me out here"*. **Please**. I should have left him right then.

This particular time, our argument was over Charlene. Yes, the Charlene who also happened to be "Charles" in Leon's phone book and who was also supposed to be a *guy* that Leon knew from school. Leon thought he was slick. The situation with Charlene really got to me because of the longevity attached to it. Initially, I didn't actually have any hard proof of what was going on between them at first, but I just *knew*. Sometimes, as a female, you just *know*. Subsequently, I found out that Leon had been in a relationship with her prior to his relationship with me. He told me that they had split up before we got together and had recently got back in contact and were now "just friends", but he was lying.

Things had been going on for a long time between them and I knew it. I would spend days upon days going over so much different things in my mind, trying to add stuff up, pondering on his whereabouts and things he'd said, and putting two and two together until I thought I was going crazy. The strange thing is, I'm not sure who I was angrier with - Leon or myself. I didn't want to admit it, but I knew from the beginning of the relationship that Charlene would be a problem, but unfortunately I ignored the warnings. I couldn't deny that Jenny had advised me to be careful from the very first day I met Leon, as well as informing me that he was meant to have a girlfriend. Yet there I was in the thick of it with Leon after going into the situation with so many red warning lights flashing, even the blind could see them.

It hurt me, because it meant that even if they *had* split up before we got together, they probably never stopped messing with each other in some sort of inappropriate way. There was no questioning it. I knew they'd been doing their thing throughout the whole of our relationship and I felt like a fool. I'd gained a beautiful son, yes, but to keep it real, it just didn't feel like *enough*. I was insecure and desperate, and these emotions fuelled me as I'd go into a blind rage and verbally belittle Leon as a defence mechanism to his name calling, accusations, and insensitivity towards me.

Now, I'd love to portray myself as being totally innocent in all of this, but that wouldn't be true. In hindsight, I accept that my behaviour was wrong. But my calculations at the time wrongly informed me that as Leon was pushing six feet tall and I was about five feet and four inches, the use of *verbal* abuse was just about all I had to fight back with. Consequently, all that would do was increase his anger, which would then result in him punching holes into my doors, walking out, and staying away for hours on end, only to then come back later and tell me he was sorry. The apologies never amounted to much, because in no time at all he would be practicing the same deceptive behaviour, and the cycle would continue, and the arguments would intensify. Unfortunately, Daniel wasn't safeguarded from this enough and would regularly be on the receiving end of our constant irresponsible behaviour.

As time went on, my entire home became a punching bag for Leon and eventually... so did I. On *those* occasions, the only reason why I stayed indoors, was not just down to being depressed, but because my face was busted from a slap or punch. But as usual, he would come around after I'd taken my key back, he'd tell me he loved me and that he didn't know why he did what he did.

He would say *"It's meeeee, babe. I'm sorry. Come on, LeeLee"* (his nick name for me, which he unwittingly didn't know was what my father called me on the few occasions I'd seen him). That would never fail at pulling on my heartstrings. He'd smile just like he did when we first met and my heart would melt. Then I would choose to believe him, but I knew deep down that I still couldn't trust him. I also wouldn't say that at that stage I'd "take him back" either, because to be honest, I don't think I ever totally or wholeheartedly left him in order to take him back.

It was a Friday. I'd been at home feeling down for days and days and had lost count of what day it was. The house was a mess, and I heard a knock at the door. Now, when you're feeling down, sometimes to even walk to the front door is a task, so I remember thinking all sorts of things:

Who is it?! What do you want? I'm not in the mood for entertaining anyone! Who is it man, cha!? I can't think now! Hang on a minute, have I paid my TV Licence?

Thankfully, it was the girlies. I hadn't been answering my phone that much all week so they organised it between themselves to meet up and come to my home uninvited. I shouldn't have been surprised because that was the norm, but my mind was all over the place. Jenny's mum had picked up Daniel for me that day, and he was spending the night at her house. I'd spoken to Jenny briefly but hadn't fully informed her about what was going on. I knew she was responsible for rallying the girls together. I kept forgetting that she knew me better than I gave her credit for.

To begin with, I wasn't in the mood. They'd brought some drinks and food with them that Esther had cooked, and happily made themselves right at home. For the next few hours, I tried my best to cheer up, but no matter how much my girls tried to keep a smile on my face, they couldn't do it. My mind kept drifting back onto how I felt - and it showed.

"Nats, I keep telling you you're too good for that dude. I dunno why you continue to put up with his constant foolishness, he ain't gonna change girl. You *know* this."

I knew Jenny was trying to be helpful, but she wasn't. I loved her, but when it came to talking to her about particular things, *especially* Leon, I didn't enjoy it. She hadn't liked him from the start, and although she never blatantly said the actual words, I could vibe when she was simply trying to say in a roundabout way "I told you so". Esther wasn't as outspoken as Jenny or Shivon on these types of topics. Instead, she would generally nod her head and agree with Jenny. Then she would find something to do. Esther liked to fix things and make things better. She was almost obsessive. When she decided to contribute to these types of discussions, what she would usually say (and all she seemed to *continuously* say that evening) was, "So what you gonna do, girl?" In response to her question, I crunched up in a ball on my sofa under my blanket with a sullen, sad, and soppy facial expression, and shrugged my shoulders like a five year old.

Shivon, on the other hand would spend most of the time on the phone rather than with the rest of us, and then randomly come out with her suggestions. This day was no different.

"Hol' on a second, bruv," she said, as she turned her attention from her phone conversation back to the rest of us. "You know what, allow him, Nats. Go find yourself a next man. Leon ain't all dat anyway. Get yourself some more options rude girl! Memba I was telling you about Justin's brother. Let me hook you up with him girl! He's buff and everyting, and you know he's liked you for tiiiiiiiiiiiiime."

I just looked at Shivon and smiled tiredly. I knew she meant well, but I just didn't know if I could be bothered with all the headache of messing around with someone else. Jenny shook her head and answered Shivon as if Shivon was suggesting this to *her*. She wasn't impressed.

"Narr, Shivon man, what's the matter with you?! She just needs to get away or something, not link another dude!"

By this time, Shivon had finished her phone conversation and was ready to verbally jump on Jenny.

"Yeah well that's alright for *you* to say, Jen. You're all wrapped up with Gavin," Shivon blurted out. "I feel sorry for that brudda. All you do is have him like a little eediat running around for you, buying your ton loads of overpriced make up. You got him wrapped 'round your little finger." Everyone began to giggle (except for Jenny). "Nats, just needs to get out there. Get that lying Leon back, instead of *him* thinking he's slick," Shivon continued.

"Whatever, Shivon. I like to look good innit; and *what*?" Jenny mumbled.

"Look good, Jen? You're obsessed!!" Shivon chuckled.

Esther came back in from the kitchen after making us a drink and tidying up a bit. She leaned her head to the side looking at me with eyes full of sympathy.

"So what you gonna do, girl?"

Here she goes with that question again.

This time I made a little more effort to respond, so not only did I shrug my shoulders again, I mustered up a "I dunno." That's about all I could say.

"You're just a hater, Shiv, that's all it is," I heard Jenny say.

Esther and I looked at each other as if to say "Here we go again". We knew that Jenny and Shivon would be debating with each other continuously for at least another hour. We left them to it, so we could have our own private conversation.

"I just don't get him, Nats; maybe you should try and talk to him." I looked at Esther wondering if she was insane.

"*Talk?* Esther this isn't Mark we're talking about you know, this is *Leon*," I said, feeling quite annoyed that she didn't get it, and secretly wishing we *were* talking about someone like Mark, because life sure would have been easier.

"There's no talking to the guy, Ess, he just loves the sound of his own voice and that's it. It's all about him," I said.

"Let's just call da gyal up innit," Shivon shouted, as she began to call Charlene a long list of derogatory names.

"No, Shiv, we've done all that stuff before man, what's the point?" Jenny argued. She was quickly losing her patience with Shivon.

"Do you want me to get Mark to talk to him?" Esther asked. I shook my head. "Well do you want something to eat then? I made your favourite, Nats. You gotta eat." Esther looked at me with pleading eyes. I shook my head again. I couldn't bear to think about food. "Well how about some vanilla ice cream then? I can go shop? I know you won't say no to that."

Once again, I shook my head.

"No ice cream, Nats?!" Esther asked, bewildered. "This is deep then."

In the background Jenny and Shivon were still going on at each other, arguing over whose suggestions for what I should do with *my* life was better.

My girlies and I spent hours talking and reminiscing on all kinds of foolishness that we'd experienced. I finally perked up a little bit and managed a few smiles. It enabled my mind to move away from what was presently happening in my life and just laugh with my girls. But the pain of my reality was like a weight in my chest that no amount of laughing could lift, and when all the jokes, laughing, and winding each other up would cease, and the bottle of wine was finished, there was a still silence between us all that was undeniable. A silence that would bring us back to the present day, and the harsh realities of what was happening. It was always the same, no matter where we were. Whoever the injured party was, whether it was Jenny, Shivon, Esther or me; the laughs would get quieter and quieter as time went on, like when the end of a song is being faded out, and then finally - a silence. Then at least one of us, if not *all* of us would inhale deeply... then exhale deeply... and stare into space.

"So what you gonna do, girl, like for real?" Esther broke the silence.

I felt exasperation rise up in me. It was directed at Esther for continuously asking me a question that I clearly didn't know how to answer, and it was also directed at myself because I felt that I should have known the answer and I didn't. Esther going on at me all the time, made me *have* to think about what I was going to do. I didn't know and I didn't want to think about it.

"I dunno, man. I'm done with him, Esther, I'm d*one*," I snapped. Of course we all knew that I didn't *technically* mean *done*. Just a fed up type of done. A "see you guys back here in a month's time" type of done. We were all used to the same unhealthy routine. I sat there quietly trying to fight back my tears.

"You coming out tomorrow?" Shivon asked. "It's Saturday man, you'll feel better for it."

Why do people talk so much rubbish sometimes? Depression doesn't just leap off of you just because it's the weekend. I had to look at my phone to even check what day it was today, and now I'm supposed to get excited because it's Saturday tomorrow? Wowee... Saturday. Nothing's leaping inside of me when I think about it. I'm not getting excited. Let me try again and say it slower: Saaaaaturdaaaaaay... Nope. Still nothing.

It was getting late. I said goodbye to the girls that evening, made arrangements with Jenny to pick up Daniel, and told them to text me when they all got home. I looked at the messy state that my bedroom was in. I sighed and trampled over everything to get to my bed, trying not to look at anything at the same time. It was as if I thought that I could sigh, and think, and wish the mess away. As I slid into bed and closed my eyes, I began to meditate. Unfortunately for me, I was meditating on the wrong things, and when you think on bad things... bad things usually follow. A person tends to pursue where their mind goes. For at least an hour, I thought about all the lies, betrayal, and disrespect I'd put up with from Leon. I felt anger begin to bubble up inside of me. I wanted to get him back. I wanted to lash out. I just wanted *something*, because moping around my house and living with dishes piled up to the (ceiling accompanied with me crying my eyes out) was not a good look anymore.

I thought about the fact that Jenny had text me and told me that she'd keep Daniel for an extra night. I thought about the fact that tomorrow was Saturday and that I could go out, and my annoyance towards Shivon's previous talk of it being Saturday was soon a distant memory. I thought about how much anticipation I had laying in my bed, an hour after the girls had left, waiting for a reply to a text I'd sent Shivon fifteen minutes earlier. Then I heard my phone beep and I read the text from Shivon.

"He's bang on it, girl! Save his number. He's gonna call you tomorrow."

I smiled mischievously and snuggled under the duvet. Justin's brother Kyle seemed like a really good prospect... Well at least at the time anyway.

LOVE'S MISCONCEPTIONS 6

Dear friends, let us continue to love one another, for love comes from God. Anyone who loves is a child of God and knows God. But anyone who does not love does not know God, for God is love.

1 John 4:7-8 (NLT)

"Muuuuuuummy, how much longer?" Daniel whined, impatiently.

"Not too long now, Son. We'll be at our stop soon."

I decided to act on Jenny's suggestion and take a much needed break. I had so much different things going on, and I needed to get away to clear my head and recuperate. I went to visit my cousin "Blue", who lived in Nottingham. Family and friends called her Blue as a nickname because she was always wearing that colour. I saw her quite frequently when we were kids, as I spent a lot of time with Nenna. Family regularly came to visit Nenna, or I would accompany Nenna on her visits to family both in and out of London. Nenna was like the rock of the family, and when she died, the family grew distant. As a result of Nenna's death, I didn't get to see Blue as much, but I tried to visit as often as I could. We had a lot in common. She was an only child, she also had a son, and she definitely understood the dynamics of my family, being part of it herself. Daniel and I had spent a couple of weeks with Blue and her son at their home in Nottingham, and were now on the train travelling back to London.

Blue and I spent loads of time catching up, reflecting, and sharing stories. Our mums had a very good relationship with each other, and they both had many similarities, so we understood each other really well. Although I thought about many things while I was away, the main thing I thought about was my mum.

Part of my reflection was on my gradual change of opinion and judgements following Mum and Desiree's argument all those years ago. I began to feel more empathy towards her, as I attempted to understand the possible reasons for some of her behaviour while I was growing up. Mum was never majorly over protective in her parenting style, but she certainly had her moments. She used to do and say some things that I never understood, but when I found out about my brother it made me look at things differently, as it began to shed light on the real motives behind some of her actions. I used to imagine what it would've been like if he were still alive, and also what it was like to lose a child in the way in which she did. I couldn't imagine it then, and I still can't imagine it now. Although I can never understand the depths of how much her loss ate away at her, I know it must have broken her heart, and I *definitely* know it affected the way she parented me.

My desire to know who she *really* was had been ongoing, but I had always felt emotionally shut off from her. I'd never been able to grasp or gain a real insight into the many activities of what I suspected to have taken place in her heart. It was as if she'd somehow managed to hide away all of her emotions into little individual compartments. Some of them she would sometimes open, and outsiders would get a snippet of how she felt, and other compartments stayed permanently closed. I'd spent a lot of energy and a lot of time resenting her for some of her actions because when I was younger my way of thinking was very simple. As far as I was concerned, parents were supposed to be faultless. It was *that* uncomplicated to me. It was *that* black and white. Parents weren't supposed to hurt you or let you down, and that was the bottom line. I had no concept of the fact that parents were actually human beings too, which meant that they had faults just like everyone else. It was probably when I hit early adulthood and began to experience life and parenthood for myself that the light switched on for me.

While we were away, on one particular night when Blue had gone to work, I had a revelation that hit me like a sledgehammer in the head. I remember putting the children to bed and watching Daniel as he slept. I went off into a bit of a daze as I gazed at my son, deep in thought. He had really misbehaved before he went to bed that evening, nevertheless, there was something about looking at him while he slept that always made my heart melt. He looked blissfully peaceful as he innocently sucked away at his thumb, totally unaware of my presence. It wasn't long before I forgot about how much he'd upset me earlier that night. What I *couldn't* shake off was the way that I handled his behaviour. I'd said things to him that I knew had hurt him, and although I gave him a hug and told him I was sorry, the damage was already done. He'd made a comment that upset me and touched a nerve. Unfortunately, I dealt with it by telling him off quite harshly and topped it off by screaming at him saying that he was just like his dad, and that he made me sick. I felt *awful*. At that time in my life, I had no real understanding of the power of my words or the negative seeds that I was sowing into his spirit, but I knew enough to admit that it was wrong. That evening I realised that, just like my mum, I wasn't a perfect parent either. I was human; I was flawed and very much in need of healing myself. I recognised straight away that those negative words had come from my own unresolved pain, confusion, and disappointment.

I cried like a baby and frantically grabbed for some tissue from the bathroom. My mascara was smudged and had got into my eyes, blurring my vision. As I cleaned my face, I took a moment to look at my reflection. I looked long and hard. As I peered at the face in the mirror, I saw something for a brief moment that startled me. It was the most bizarre and interesting thing – I saw my mum's face looking back at me. I jumped back. Then I looked at my reflection again and began to think.

I thought about what I'd said to Daniel again. It was like an echo of words I'd heard Mum say to me when I was a similar age. It was like hearing an old song playing that you remember from your childhood; only it was a song that you didn't like. Those words were just the kind of words she'd use to indirectly display her bitterness and resentment towards my absent father. But my father wasn't around for her to spew her verbal poison at – so I guess I was the next best thing.

You're just like your dad. He had a nasty attitude and so do you…

I didn't like her for it, and I resented my dad for it, because apparently I was behaving like someone who I'd only met a few times and never had a relationship with. There I was, battling with attributes of my personality that I didn't like and couldn't pin-point their origin, yet Mum wouldn't miss the opportunity to point out exactly where they came from and there seemed to be nothing I could do about them. It hurt and puzzled me at the time, and it hurt me that evening at Blue's house because it was clear to me that I was hurting my son.

I sat there staring at him, as I thought about dysfunctional behavioural patterns that travel down generations of families going unnoticed (or ignored). I also wondered if Mum ever had similar thoughts to me, or ever felt this way about her relationship with Nenna. I considered how many aspects of *her* mindset were picked up from Nenna and how many things I had picked up from her. I also realised that hurting people – hurt people. It's not an excuse for mistreatment, but it's certainly a reality; especially where no real healing has taken place.

I also began to feel guilty for having so many different negative and confusing thoughts and feelings towards Mum when deep down, despite all of the mistakes she made, a lot of the time she was acting out of love. By this I mean that she was loving me the only way *she* knew how to. *Her* idea and understanding of love was based on a mixture of different aspects of *her* life, *her* upbringing, *her* surroundings, *her* experiences and perceptions. Whether right or wrong in anyone's opinion, that was all she knew, and *my* perception of love was based on the same things.

This is the case for a lot of us and unfortunately we are left with a severely warped and distorted concept of what real love actually is. I spent my whole life having viewed and experienced so many definitions of that word, that by the time I was in my early twenties I was just plain old confused because *everyone* had their *own* version of it. Family, friends, strangers, significant others, and myself of course. Everyone seemed to consciously or subconsciously have their own set of rules. So if everyone had their *own* set of rules, I had to wonder what *real* love truly was.

Let me give you an example. When it came to the type of love projected in romantic relationships, I mainly used to come to negative conclusions about what it was and what it could potentially mean for me, due to what I was exposed to. I would hear snippets of conversations like, *"He doesn't love you otherwise he wouldn't have done that to you"*. Or I would hear some heartbroken soul saying, *"He told me he loved me then he done this to me, which means he never loved me in the first place"*, surrounded by other people either agreeing or disagreeing. To add to this, I'd then read something somewhere or see something on the television, or think about the many comments I'd heard about my dad over the years, which would add fuel to the fire. From all of these conclusions (with my own experiences added), I didn't realise that I had subconsciously created my own little personal definition of what that type of love meant - not even considering for a split second that it wasn't necessarily true.

I didn't consider the fact that I was *just* like everyone else. I was making *true*, what was really just down to opinion, because the fact is that what love means to "Suzie" doesn't necessarily mean the same thing to "Sally". Yet sometimes we take other peoples words and advice and ideas on board and accept it as the truth, then ignorantly apply it to our own lives without looking at the bigger picture.

Let's take these two best friends "Suzie" and "Sally". If Suzie believes that the type of love exercised and expressed in a romantic relationship should mean that a man must buy you clothes and jewellery in abundance, and if he doesn't, then that means that he doesn't love you and he's not worth entertaining, does that mean she's correct? Suzie's friend Sally may say yes, after years of her best friend Suzie projecting this opinion onto her when sharing her opinions. Then unfortunately for Sally, she may be influenced by this, resulting in her possibly taking on this mindset and acting on it. What Sally doesn't realise is that Suzie was raised by an extremely superficial and materialistic mother who put a price tag on her own personal value, which her husband (Suzie's father) also reinforced. He expressed *his* version of love by buying her the best things that money could buy as a substitute for spending time with her and the family; therefore passing this mentality down to Suzie; and on and on the poisonous cycle goes with the enemy succeeding in deceiving the masses. The good news for me was realising that the poisonous cycle stops when Jesus

Christ intervenes.

The truth of the matter is that if we don't know who Jesus Christ is and haven't experienced *His* love, then no matter how intelligent, street-wise, experienced in life, educated or well informed that we *think* we are, we haven't experienced the true and full essence of what *real* love is. That's the bottom line. I am so thankful that I've now realised and I'm still experiencing this truth, and only wished I'd realised it sooner. Jesus *is* love. God *is* love. It begins with Him *first*.

Every time I reflect on all the impulsive decisions and irresponsible, misguided seasons of my earlier years, I wonder what would have happened and where I would have ended up if it wasn't for God's grace and love covering me and keeping me. I can truthfully and wholeheartedly say, the place wouldn't have been pretty.

"Mum, Mum, everyone's getting up! Are we there now?" Daniel yelled.

"Yes, Dandans, this is our stop baby," I said sighing heavily, disappointed that our break was over. "Let's go home, Son."

Oh What A Tangled Web We Weave...

The wisdom of the wise keeps life on track; the foolishness of fools lands them in the ditch.

Proverbs 14:8 (MSG)

"Look, I love you, Leelee. You know it's not like that with them other girls. It's just a physical thing with them. Babes, you know how I get. My mum just got under my skin after she came round, and I started thinking about things. I felt angry innit. You weren't talking to me so, boy... I just... look I flopped innit."

That was Leon's version of an apology and explanation which he gave to me some time after I got back from my break. He was also trying to convince me that he wasn't talking to Charlene anymore, and after giving me some half-baked apology he sat there impatiently waiting for me to respond. What added to his frustration was my previous reluctance to answer any of his calls. I wasn't interested in speaking to him at the time, so I ignored him. I'd taken back my keys from him before I went away, and had no intention of giving them back.

After a few weeks of receiving the silent treatment from me, he tried to get to me through Daniel. This was his usual and very predictable routine. He would say, *"I wanna see my son! You're tryna take me for some kind of fool, Natalie, but it's cool 'cause watch what I'm gonna do; and I tell you what, don't make me find out you got any next man around my son, 'cause I'll buss ya head!! Don't play with me, Natalie!!"*

I didn't care much for Leon and his threats. Admittedly, I was scared of him at times because he had a temper, but at that moment in time I was completely fed up of him and disinterested in anything he had to say or do. He continued to talk, but my mind shut off. I was looking directly at him as he spoke, but instead of listening, I lip read his words because everything he was saying sounded like waffle and he was giving me a headache.

Bla, bla, bla, Leon. I don't care!! What are you gonna do, really? Cheat again? I'm already used to that. Slap me, or punch me? Been there done that too. As far as I'm concerned, there's not much more you CAN do.

So there I was, resentfully attempting to look interested in what he had to say, and as much as I'd anticipated this conversation, when it was actually happening I wasn't really feeling it. I was tired. Mentally tired.

"Are you listening to me, babes? I said I flopped innit ... I'm sorry," Leon said, looking at me as though he expected his words to miraculously make everything better. I looked at Leon, blank faced and unresponsive, and sharply grunted, "Hmm." That was it. I went to my room to be by myself, leaving him and Daniel to play, wrestle, and mess up my front room with their games and antics. It was really bright outside so I drew my curtains, lay down on my bed, and switched on the television to distract myself from my feelings because I didn't want to be sucked in by Leon again.

I must have fallen asleep because when I felt Leon tapping on my shoulder and I looked up and out of the window, it was dark outside. I sat up rubbing my eyes, feeling slightly disorientated and still a bit sleepy, asking Leon where Daniel was.

"Don't worry about Dandans, I put him to bed innit," Leon said.

My mind started doing its usual maternal check list. "Yeah but did he -"

"*Yes,* Nats. He had his dinner," Leon interrupted.

"What about -"

"Nats, cooool man!" Leon stopped me mid-sentence again. "Don't you think I know how to look after my son? I done told you bare times, my paps done a good job with me man!"

"Okay, Leon!" I snapped. "I was just checking."

It was a common thing for Leon to get defensive. He wasn't exactly father of the year, but he made the effort as and when he felt like it. He was very selective about when he chose to take up his responsibilities as a father. I knew that he "loved" Daniel in his own mixed up way, but he had a whole load of unresolved issues that affected the way he related to me, to Daniel, to women, and with people in general.

Leon's mum walked out on him, his younger brother, and their father when he was a child. For many years, she didn't make contact. She returned without warning when Leon and his brother were in their teens, and had persistently tried to re-establish a relationship with them. I didn't know why she initially left, and every time I tried to bring the subject up with Leon he would fob me off, or get really irritated about it. On other occasions, I'd hear him try and make a joke out of it, but I knew that deep down he didn't find it funny and his attempt to laugh it off was a cover up. I decided, after several times of asking Leon why she left, that it was better for me to not bring it up again. I sometimes wondered whether he was actually aware of the reason, or if he ever spoke to his dad about it. Although he had a really good relationship with his dad, I didn't know the ins and outs of the situation. I made my peace with the fact that Leon spoke about those kinds of things as and when he chose, and also *how* he chose. He didn't like to be interrogated or pushed.

When Leon's mum (Maxine) came back into his life, they spoke sporadically; but although he had *some* form of relationship with her, it was still strained. Maxine would try to reach out to Leon in numerous ways, and would sometimes invite him to her house, but Leon was guarded and standoffish. Understandably, he struggled with the whole thing.

When I gave birth to Daniel, Maxine really tried to make an effort. Sometimes she would invite us to her house for dinner, or she'd come to visit Daniel at the hostel where I lived before I moved into my flat. I can recall one evening when I was at her house with Daniel. Leon had said that he would meet us there because he had a few things to do before the end of the day. Maxine was preparing a huge dinner for us, we'd been there for a while, and Leon still hadn't arrived. We waited and waited. I called Leon and I text Leon, but to no avail. I felt so disappointed for Maxine. We made small talk and she spent a lot of time bonding with Daniel and getting to know him. We watched a film and had woman to woman type conversations, but I could see her anxiously watching the clock throughout the whole time. It was awkward. No one really wanted to admit it but we both knew that Leon wasn't coming. When a few hours had passed, she plastered on a smile that didn't succeed in covering the disappointment she was feeling, and said in an unconvincing high pitched tone, "Let's eat, Natalie." After we'd eaten I received a text from Leon saying he'd be there soon. Leon didn't turn up that day, and he continued to do the same thing. It went on for years.

"Babes, you look tired. Do you want anything? If not, I wanna go play some computer before I duck out?" Leon said, trying to stay in my good books.

I shook my head and lay back down, still feeling sleepy. He bent down to kiss me but I was reluctant. I really wanted to believe Leon this time, but I knew it was the same old talk, and I was always falling for it.

When Leon bent down to kiss me on my cheek, something that was placed on the floor at the other end of my room made me snap straight out of the sleepy state I was in. I shot up like the house was on fire, with my stomach tying in knots. I was reluctant to respond to Leon before, but in my state of panic I decided to grab him quickly so that he wouldn't turn around; and all the while my eyes were transfixed on what I could see on the floor at the back of my bedroom. I hugged Leon and tried to drag the hug out for as long as I could, mainly because I was trying to figure out what to do. Unfortunately, Leon thought that the hug was an invitation to try and take it a step further, but that was the *last* thing on my mind. I could feel my heart pounding as if it was going to burst through my chest. I was panicking trying to think… and fast.

Come on Natalie think, think, THINK!! If he finds out what's going on it's over for you. THINK!!

I'm sure the whole thing only lasted for a few minutes in reality, but it felt like a lifetime. All of a sudden the house phone rang. Leon tried to get me to ignore it, but what Leon didn't understand was that, the phone ringing at that second was like God handing me a life line. I answered the phone and it was Leon's brother. Leon didn't want to take the call because his mind was on other things, but I told him that I needed to go to the toilet. Obviously, I didn't really need to go to the toilet but I needed to get to the far end of my bedroom - sharpish. He was agitated and grabbed the phone.

"Yes, bruv! What's up?" he barked.

I watched Leon closely as I walked down to the end of my bedroom. By this time, he was distracted by the conversation he was having, so with my eyes still stuck on him, I took my foot and quickly kicked my dressing gown over the Nike cap that was on the floor. I didn't make a good job of it initially because I was too busy watching Leon. Still panicking, I then kicked the partially covered cap behind the chair in my room before Leon realised what I was doing. When I kicked the cap I noticed that a chain was underneath it. I nearly fell over in shock and fear. I desperately wanted the floor to cave in, but I kept my eyes slyly glued to Leon. I moved swiftly, and finally managed to kick everything behind the chair with the cap and chain fully out of sight. There was no way that I could afford for Leon to lay his eyes on them. If he had, only God knows what would've happened, or what I could have possibly said to convince him to believe any of the lies that I would've told.

The problem with the cap and chain was that they didn't belong to Leon. They belonged to Kyle. He'd left them there the night before. I'd been unwise and started seeing Kyle since Shivon gave him my number. I quickly snuck out of the bedroom to pretend to go to the toilet, before Leon wondered what I was doing. I didn't feel too clever as I sat on the toilet with my head in my hands. I was breathing as though I just ran the marathon. A million things raced through my mind and I couldn't think straight.

What are you DOING Natalie? Are you silly? Leon will kill you, and is this thing with Kyle even what you want? Why are you doing this?

I had got myself into a mess. A big mess. In fact, I was in such a nervous and anxious state, that I ended up doing a pee for real.

ALL THAT GLITTERS ISN'T GOLD 8

But every person is tempted when he is drawn away, enticed and baited by his own evil desire (lust, passions).

James 1:14 (AMP)

I looked at the wad of twenty pound notes in my hand and pondered. I looked at Kyle, then back at the money and continued to ponder.

"Just take it, Natalie. You said you needed some stuff for you and little man so what's the problem?" Kyle said, trying to reassure me. He smiled.

Kyle your smile is soooooo nice. Nothing like Leon's... but it's close...

"I dunno, Kyle... it's a bit much innit," I answered, shrugging my shoulders and staring at the money in my hands.

"Well I ain't taking it back so, bwoy. Man like me might start to get offended and ting..." Kyle smiled again, and was not taking no for an answer.

He leaned forward and gave me a long, slow, kiss on the forehead. I closed my eyes and tried to embrace the feeling of comfort it gave me. I felt warm and mushy on the inside. My tense posture began to relax. As he pulled away, I quickly opened my eyes and sat up straight before he noticed my mushy demeanour.

Kyle got up from beside me and went into his kitchen to finish cooking. I sat and watched him in astonishment as he prepared about enough food to feed the five thousand. I couldn't believe how big his appetite was, and had no idea where all his food went. Kyle was tall and medium built, but his size definitely didn't reflect the amount of food he could put away in one day. I decided to confront him about his level of food consumption.

"I can't believe you're eating *more* food after you already stuffed your face at the restaurant!"

"What you talking about? That just lined my stomach, Nats, man. Whad'you take this ting for? Man's gotta eat you na!" Kyle said, in between laughing and choking on his spliff. "I gotta take care of myself you know, Nats. Anyway... do you want summa this?"

"Narr I'm cool," I said, trying to sound extra polite. Kyle wasn't the best cook in the world and I didn't want to hurt his feelings.

"What?... You dissin mans cooking skills then?" he asked jokingly before he began his dismal attempt at acting, pretending that he was heartbroken.

I laughed so much that I had to catch my breath before I responded. "*Skills?* What is it with you guys? You think that just 'cause you can make a little tuna and pasta, that makes you a top notch chef. It's just tuna and pasta, Kyle!"

Within seconds we were in fits of laughter which was interrupted by the sound of my mobile phone's piercing ring tone. I irritably picked up the phone, looked at the name on the screen, and switched the phone off without answering it.

"Who was dat, Nat?" Kyle asked, coming out of the kitchen.

"No one," I said abruptly.

Kyle smiled. *He knew who it was.*

"You know that eediat don't deserve you, right? I aint liked that guy from day. He's a fool."

Kyle had made it painfully obvious that he didn't like Leon. He didn't know him personally, but had mainly heard about him and seen him around from time to time. Apparently, one of Kyle's friends had an altercation with Leon some years ago, and Kyle disliked him from then. In fact, quite a few people didn't like Leon because he was quite arrogant and he had a big mouth. To add to this, Leon was also what some may say "doing well for himself" financially at the time and I think a lot of his peers were jealous.

I swiftly changed the subject. I didn't want to talk or think about Leon. "You know what, thanks for this, Kyle," I said coyly, putting the wad of money he gave me into my bag.

"Dat's cool babe, it's *nothing*," Kyle said, reassuring me. After eating his food, he sat down beside me and opened his arms really wide, waiting for me to hug him. A hug was just what I needed as the mention of Leon's name started to dampen my mood. Kyle and I leaned back into his sofa, held each other tightly and lay there in silence. The only thing I could hear was the sound of his heartbeat as I shut my eyes and put my head to rest on his chest.

Kyle and I had an enjoyable day together. Daniel was with my mum so I'd spent the whole day with Kyle. While we were out, he made a few stops at his friend's houses that lived out of the area, which I felt quite uncomfortable about at the time (even though I stayed in the car). I was wary of people seeing me with him in case word got back to Leon somehow. I knew Kyle and Leon weren't friends, but as we all know - people talk; and if Leon found out, it would have been over for me. I was taking a big risk with Kyle. We went out shopping far away from the area, and spent lots of time making each other laugh and messing around. Later on that day we went to watch a film that I was eager to see, had something to eat, and came back to his place. He also caught on to how much I liked vanilla ice cream, and he took me to some ice cream parlour that made the best Italian ice cream I'd had in years. Again it has to be said, it wasn't as good as the ice cream Nenna used to get for me - but it was close.

I also had a few errands to run during the day and Kyle was constantly putting his hand in his pocket. Although I didn't expect him to, I liked the fact that he would always offer. He was thoughtful and I liked the way it made me feel. We were both aware that I had my own money, even if it wasn't a lot, but Kyle liked to spoil me and I didn't complain. His behaviour was always the same; if I happened to mention in passing that I needed something, without a doubt Kyle would be calling me the next day with either a brand new version of what I'd said I needed or some form of suggestion or solution to fix my problem. He was cool. It reminded me of the earlier days of mine and Leon's relationship. Unfortunately, Leon had grown to be very tight with his money over the years, and very inconsistent with supporting Daniel.

After some time had passed, Kyle broke the silence. We were still slumped in the sofa wrapped up in each other's arms.

"Maaaaaaaaan... you're nuff pretty innit?"

I looked up, and he was staring at me as if it was the first time he'd seen me. I smiled awkwardly and giggled a little bit. I felt embarrassed. I didn't know why, I just didn't really know how to respond.

"You're not used to hearing dem kynna tings are you?" Kyle asked inquisitively. "It's like, every time I say something like that to you, you get all bashful."

"Yeah I am used to it, it's just weird innit. I get all shy and that," I lied. I felt like an idiot. I wanted the floor to swallow me up. It had nothing to do with me being shy, I just wasn't used to hearing those kind of words spoken to me and couldn't pin point how it made me feel. All I knew was that my insides would squirm each and every time. Kyle was always telling me how nice I looked and how well I did things, and although it felt strange to receive the compliments, it was nice to hear. It had been a really long time since I'd heard anything positive about myself from anyone besides my girls.

Kyle was still looking at me and I didn't know what to say, so I hung my head down. The atmosphere began to feel tense. Kyle was trying to figure me out. I looked up at him for a split second but looked down again, trying to avoid eye contact. Kyle took his hand, gently touched my chin and lifted it up so he could see my face properly. I moved my face away, but he gently moved it back to face him again. He looked at me straight in the eye. I felt his eyes piercing into me as though he could see straight into my soul. I felt awkward, vulnerable, and transparent.

What's the matter with me?

Kyle cupped my face in his hands and I felt my stomach do something funny again. I looked to the left, then to the right, then to the floor, then to the top of his head and back to the floor again. I looked *everywhere* apart from his eyes.

"*Look* at me, Natalie," Kyle said seriously. I couldn't do it. I felt knots tying in my belly every other second and then a sudden overwhelming need to cry.

Uh oh… don't even think about crying! I can't afford to look all weak and dumb in front of this guy! What's the matter with me?!

"*Look* at me, Natalie," Kyle whispered firmly. There was nowhere else for me to look, so I closed my eyes. I felt like a child. "You're beautiful, Nat. *You're beautiful.*"

I remained silent, but deep inside of me I was screaming at the top of my lungs:

"Stop lying!! I'm not beautiful, I'm just ME. STOP LYING TO ME!!"

I felt a warm tear fall slowly onto my cheek. It was warm and gradually fell onto my lip. I felt Kyle's finger wipe it away. It relaxed me. I felt scared but I wasn't sure why. My heart was beating ridiculously fast.

What is WRONG with me?!

I don't remember at what point we fell asleep, but I do remember that Kyle had made me feel a mixture of different emotions that evening… some of which I didn't understand, and it stuck with me for a long time. It was the first time he'd seen me so vulnerable. I also realised that night how much I liked him but we both knew that I was still wrapped up in Leon, and although I knew that Leon had cheated on me time after time, I still didn't want him finding out about what I was doing. God knows what he would say or do. Initially, I thought I didn't care about him knowing, but I did. I also knew that I wasn't the only person Kyle was seeing, but to be honest, I didn't really care about that either. He didn't want a relationship and I wasn't looking for one with him. All I wanted was for Leon to change. I figured he owed me. I was looking for "love". I was expecting someone with unresolved issues, someone who hit me and disrespected me, to *love* me. Then to make matters worse, I was messing around with someone else who told me all the things I wanted to hear, yet slept with other people and didn't want to commit, and yet somehow… *somehow* I genuinely believed that I would reap positivity out this mixed up madness. I honestly did.

As I continued to see Kyle, things between him and I remained calm and drama free and we both seemed happy enough with our arrangement. I stayed away from Leon for a while but as always, started the usual on and off thing with him. As time went on I also began to see a change in my attitude and behaviour. I started to feel empowered (although I wasn't) when it came to how I dealt with Leon. When Leon and I would argue, I found myself being just that little bit more loud mouthed than usual. I got brave. I would continuously and casually ignore his calls, and if he didn't make the effort to call me, I wasn't as bothered as I used to be. I didn't care if I heard from Leon from one day to the next. I saw it as progress, but it wasn't - it was deception. The only reason I behaved this way was because I was involved with Kyle, and I got a kick out of knowing what I was doing. It was almost as if I thought I had some secret weapon or something. When I would hear from different people about Leon's shenanigans and his interactions with different females, I can't deny that it still hurt. But then I'd think about what I had with Kyle and misguidedly tried to use the thought to take the edge off the pain. It was really unhealthy, and it also didn't work. I also can't say that at this point in my life I was truly happy or content because I wasn't. Even when I thought I was, I knew I was kidding myself and I knew I needed *something*, I just didn't know what.

Every now and again, I would still cry myself to sleep and still imagine God giving me a hug but I figured that God must've given up on me. I continued to search for various ways of numbing my thoughts, feelings, and pain, but they were all temporal and ineffective. I had my up days and down days, but felt more "up" most of the time, so that was an improvement in *my* book. Months flew by like they were days and I started to think more about my future. Eventually I reduced my hours at work so that I could go back to college to study. Unfortunately I missed out on enrolment the year before because I was at home with a badly busted lip after an argument with Leon, so I was too embarrassed to step foot into the college.

This year was different, and although things were not perfect, I was just glad that for the moment, there wasn't any drama. Generally, I'd felt better than I had done in months. Things were looking better for me, I smiled more often, and everybody noticed. The funny thing about life though, is that it has an unavoidable way of changing, and little did I know that it was only a matter of time before the smile on my face would *totally* disappear.

MIND THE GAP 9

Jesus replied 'Love the lord with all your heart and with all your soul and with all your mind. This is the greatest commandment. And the second is like it, love your neighbour as yourself'

Matthew 22: 37-39 (NIV)

And in Christ you have been brought to fullness...

Colossians 2:10 (NIV)

Getting involved with Kyle was another number in a long list of unwise choices. I thank God for enabling me to learn from the unwise decisions I made, but like I've mentioned before, I still sometimes wonder what would've happened if God's grace wasn't available. I was so wrapped up in unhealthy mindsets and deeply embedded in brokenness, that I would never have been able to see my way through. I have no doubt that I would have continued to travel down a destructive path, and satan wouldn't have missed out on the opportunity of giving me a helping hand at destroying myself. As I reflect on this I cringe, but I also smile because now I can see what I couldn't see before.

One of the first revelations I had when I began my journey with Jesus, was one that sounds simple, but not always easy to put into practice. It was that I can't change *anyone*. I'm totally aware of how obvious this sounds, but it's amazing how much time and energy I invested in trying to change things about other people that were never *my* job to change.

I believe that in some situations, a woman's natural nurturing side can take over and she either consciously or subconsciously believes that she can change her significant other. The truth is that she can't. We are responsible for our *own* growth. Unfortunately, it's when we start thinking that we can change an individual that we end up setting ourselves up for being disappointed. This happens when we place *our* hopes and expectations of a person onto them. I don't believe there is anything wrong with having desires and standards; but something to consider is that, although we may want something *for* or *from* an individual - Do they want the same thing? *Should* they want the same thing? Maybe... maybe not. I guess it depends on what the situation is. I learned the hard way, that the best thing to do is to seek God's will, His wisdom, His plan and direction in everything (including relationships), because whether it turns out the way that we envisioned or not, His will is *always* best.

Before I learned this lesson, I continued to make this mistake with Leon. I thought that all I needed to do was look after him and show him that I loved him as much as I could, and everything would be cool. It was a very naive and misguided outlook. I had wrongly concluded that because Leon's relationship with his mum had negatively affected him, I could by some means fix it. How was I going to do that exactly? Number one, it wasn't my responsibility. I don't have or ever will have the ability to heal the wounded spirit of another person, because only God can do that. Number two, I didn't even love myself the way I should have! I thought I did, but I didn't. Leon didn't love himself very much either. So how were either of us supposed to give to each other what we didn't even have for ourselves?

Here's an analogy: If I asked you for some chewing gum and you didn't have any, how are you supposed to give me any? You wouldn't be able to give me what you didn't have, even if you wanted to. The only way you'd be able to would be if you went to get some first. I have come to find that love isn't that much different.

I learned that there's an order to this love thing. God requires us to love Him first and foremost, and *then* to love our neighbour *as we love ourselves*, but if we are not acquainted with real love *none* of it can happen. Firstly, God *is* love. If we don't have a relationship with God, there's no way of knowing what real love actually is. Subsequently, if we don't know *His* love, we're unable to love ourselves *correctly*. And if we don't love ourselves correctly, how on earth can we expect to effectively love anyone else?

The society we live in promotes the idea of being fulfilled, satisfied, and complete through everything else *but* Christ. Society says that the solution for fulfilment comes through yourself, your relationships, your own resources, or someone else's. It influences, seduces, and deceives people into thinking that they become complete in things and people. This is not the truth because Jesus completes us. God made us; He's our manufacturer, so if something is broken it's *His* job to fix it. In Him we are complete. In a relationship between a man and woman, it should never be two halves coming together, but two *whole* people coming together to share a life journey in partnership through the empowerment, grace, and guidance of Jesus Christ. We can't become whole by our own strength and ability; it doesn't work that way. Sadly, as I was one of those "halves" on entering a relationship with Leon, I indirectly looked to him to fill voids that were never going to be sustainable or achievable because it wasn't his responsibility to fill them. So, when Leon began to disappoint and not give me what I thought I needed from him, I sought it elsewhere. That's how I ended up messing around with Kyle.

Kyle was what I saw as my knight in shining armour for the season I was in. He was my man of the hour. He was smooth, looked good, and listened to what I had to say. Kyle was thoughtful and made me feel good about myself. Of course, I shouldn't have needed him or anyone else to make me feel good about myself, but that's how my mind worked at the time. I didn't know who I truly was, and I didn't know *whose* I was, so anything went. I had no idea about who I was in Christ and had no relationship with Him as my Creator, so a bunch of junk, culture, and ever changing standards of society defined me as a person. I didn't stand for anything, so I fell for anything. Kyle became my emotional version of a builder. He took out the polyfilla and filled gaps and cracks in where my soul was crushed and damaged. But the thing is that when you fill in cracks and paint over them so they can't be seen, although everything *looks* as good as new, the cracks (whether filled with polyfilla or not) are still underneath. Jesus doesn't work that way. He doesn't make things *as good as* new, He makes all things new - if you let him.

Until I had this revelation, Kyle was the one who told me all the things that I wanted to hear, and that was what I held on to. He was filling a gap that Leon wasn't filling in my life and heart anymore. Thankfully, I now realise that both situations with Kyle and Leon were a subconscious attempt on my part to spiritually fill the void that Jesus Christ was always meant to fill.

To expect a man (whether he is your husband or not) to fill the place of Jesus Christ, is like expecting a square peg to fill a circular hole. Yes, a man can and will satisfy you on a natural level, so let's just be honest and real about that. A man can be there to hold us, provide for us, support us, love us, and wipe away our tears, but a man doesn't have the capacity to heal our deep pain, or mend our broken spirits. The most he can do is love us through it and hold our hands. Wholeness is a journey, but one that we can only go on with two passengers - ourselves and God. It's a journey that I'm still on and still learning about, and one of the lessons learned is this: Brokenness plus brokenness equals a recipe for disaster.

While I'm talking about recipes, let me throw this question out there (it may seem random but it's relevant). Would you eat a cake that someone gave to you, which was made with rotten eggs and out of date ingredients and expect to not get a bellyache? I'm guessing you wouldn't. The cake may even look great and might even initially taste okay, so it may seem like after you've taken a bite, you're okay. However, sooner or later the cake is going to make you feel sick, whether you blame it on the cake or not. The cake *seemed* okay and it certainly *looked* okay otherwise you wouldn't have eaten it... but that's part of the problem... that's part of the trick. satan (the devil, the enemy, the accuser... take your pick) is an expert in offering things to us that *look* fantastic, but when we take a bite after being deceived, the consequences are dangerous and certainly not so sweet. When I think about the fruit that was offered to Eve in the Garden of Eden, I imagine it looked amazing too, and the prospect of eating it seemed like a good idea at the time. Didn't mean it was, though. The trick was the same in the Garden of Eden when the devil tempted Eve, and it's still the same to this day.

I continued to see Kyle on and off for a long time, never really feeling one hundred per cent at peace with the idea. Every time I thought about it I would try and convince myself that I was justified in my actions:

Leon's treating me badly, and I have every reason to do what I'm doing. I mean, look at the things that he does!

Those were the type of statements I'd come up with. I never saw that the only person that I was treating badly was *myself*. I was hurting *myself*. Sleeping with and emotionally feeding from Kyle wasn't doing anyone any favours. It was certainly affecting me and damaging my spirit in more ways than I realised.

My friends more or less backed me up in my destructive decisions. And even for the friends who didn't, their rationale sounded good but it wasn't based on real substance. I don't blame them because they were only speaking from where they were in their lives at that time, and what they knew. They couldn't give me substance because just like me, they didn't have any substance (once again, they couldn't give me what they didn't have for themselves so the principle is the same as before).

Nevertheless, we were all operating out of some form of dysfunction, but they all looked different. Every one of us, whether male or female, had our different "cakes" along with our different masks to cover them up. satan offered many a cake and mask to us. Some came in the shape of smoking or drugs; another was promiscuity or experimenting with ones sexuality. Another was obsession with body image. There was also over-eating or intentionally not eating enough. Others were, hiding behind bravado, keeping busy, over achieving, obsession with money and material gain or status. Then there was the need to always be in a relationship, or the guys who thought that the more girls they had, the better kind of man they were. The list was endless and very varied. Some were covert and others were overt, and we certainly didn't see it for what it was. They were all devices of the enemy, but don't be fooled, they were and still are *very* real.

For this season of my life, Kyle was my cake. My cake *seemed* good and undoubtedly *looked* good, so just like Eve... I ate it.

WHO CAN'T HEAR MUST FEEL 10

They rejected my advice and paid no attention when I cor-
rected them. Therefore, they must eat the bitter fruit of living
their own way, choking on their own schemes. For simpletons
turn away from me—to death. Fools are destroyed by their own
complacency. But all who listen to me will live in peace, untrou-
bled by fear of harm.

Proverbs 1:30-33 (NLT)

I stood in the same spot for what seemed like forever, looking at different pictures of Mum in the living room. I gazed at old pictures of
myself, and ones of Mum when she was a baby. We looked so much
alike, it was quite uncanny. I began to wonder if Mum and I had many personality similarities when we were both small children. I analysed every
picture and wandered off into deep thought while each individual picture
told a different story. I studied each picture in chronological order, and
was humoured and fascinated by the different changes in Mum's facial
features and body shape over the years. I was amazed at how gracefully
she'd evolved from childhood to womanhood. The only things that hadn't
changed much were her eyes. Her eyes had a deepness about them. Her
eye colour was a deep rich brown, but had a slight touch of hazel around
the edges of her irises. They were stunning. When you looked at her they
were the first thing that you noticed because they were piercing, bright,
and extraordinary. But it you looked close enough, if you paid a lot of attention to them, you could see the pain hidden away in them at the same
time. Her eyes told a story all by themselves.

"Nat!!" Mum shouted.

"Yeah?" I shouted back. A minute went by and Mum still hadn't replied. "Yes, Mum?!" I shouted again in frustration.

Silence.

Why do you do that Mum? Call me and then go silent? I really can't stand it.

I reluctantly decided to go upstairs to see what she wanted. I strolled into her bedroom and stood there watching her as she dragged out one of Daniel's puzzles from the bottom of her wardrobe for him to play with. "*Yes,* Mum?" I asked for what seemed to be the millionth time.

"Go and get Dandans a packet of crisps from out of the cupboard, and a Ribena out of the fridge please."

I was annoyed because I didn't see why Mum or Daniel couldn't have done it themselves. I thought it was a complete waste of my time going all the way upstairs, just to hear that. I stomped downstairs with thoughts running through my mind that I didn't have the energy or bravery to verbalise:

Why didn't you tell me what you wanted in the first place, Mum? I could've got them before I came upstairs, but now I have to make a double trip. Where's the logic? Actually, why can't you get them yourself? Cha! These stairs are draining me.

I only had to travel up one flight of stairs, but I felt tired. Daniel was ransacking the place as usual but Mum just left him to it. She spoiled Daniel. She was definitely more affectionate towards him than she was towards me when I was his age. Sometimes I felt weird about it, but at the same time I loved the fact that they were close. Maybe it had something to do with the loss of her son. I don't know. When those thoughts came into my mind, it hurt because I'd think to myself, "*You still have ME Mum, I'M still here*". Nevertheless, I was grateful that Daniel was experiencing some of the same things with his nan that I was blessed enough to share with Nenna before she died.

After reluctantly getting Daniel's snacks, I dragged myself back up-

WHO CAN'T HEAR MUST FEEL

stairs and helped Mum put her new shoe rack together. After that, we spent hours going through old clothes that she was planning on throwing out. She'd recently changed jobs and decided that she wanted to do a spring clean. She had newly re-decorated her room and it looked fresh and vibrant. She'd chosen light and neutral colours that really complemented the rest of the house. I looked at her new furniture and felt inspired.

Maybe I should re-decorate? My place could do with it. Then again, would Leon ever get round to it? Knowing him, he'd probably get some of his people to start it and then he'd fall out with them and leave the work half finished. Maybe not then.

I looked at Mum's exercise bike and laughed. "What you laughing at, Mum?" Daniel asked.

"I'm laughing at your nan," I chuckled.

"Yeah but she's not in here, she's gone toilet," Daniel smartly pointed out.

"Don't worry about it, Dans."

I was laughing because the exercise bike was once a treasured present that Mum cared for and used religiously. But now, it was covered with dresses, trousers, and cardigans. Mum had even gone one step further to express her creative skills, by using the handles of the bike to shove her many bangles and bracelets on. I laughed again to myself, shook my head, and sat down for a few minutes. All of the spring cleaning and D.I.Y. stuff was taking its toll on me. I wondered where Mum had got to, and saw her outside talking to the neighbours next door when I looked through her bedroom window. Mum's neighbours were fond of Daniel, and were outside handing some toys over to her which they had bought back from their holiday break. Daniel saw the toys in Mum's hands and knew straight away that they were for him.

"Can I go get them, Mum? Pleaaaase, Mum?"

"Okay, Daniel. Gosh, you don't miss *anything* do you?" I laughed.

Daniel jumped on me and gave me a big kiss before racing out the door. I slightly pushed him away because the smell of cocoa butter cream on his face was too strong and made me feel queasy.

After having a good laugh at some of Mum's "back in the day" garments, I sat down and watched the television for a while and waited for her to come back upstairs.

Now I know she's not expecting me to sort through all of her stuff by myself. Don't be expecting to spend forever outside talking, then come back in and start complaining about feeling tired. I love you Mum, but you're not getting away with it today.

After watching one of my favourite talk shows, I realised that Mum still hadn't come back upstairs, but I had been so engrossed in the television that I hadn't even noticed, and I also didn't know what Daniel was doing either. I decided to go downstairs to see where everyone had disappeared to. Mum was standing in the living room holding a picture of her and Nenna, totally transfixed. She was completely unaware that I was standing by the door watching her, and when she realised I was there, she hurriedly put the picture down, looking a little bit like a child who'd been caught with their fingers in the cookie jar. She then began to tidy up the living room when it was clear that it didn't need tidying up. I wanted to ask her about the picture and what she was thinking about while she was looking at it, but I didn't.

She looked at me strangely, just as she'd done when I first arrived at the house, but I didn't ask her what the look was about *then*, and I wasn't about to ask her now. You could never tell what was going on through her mind and I didn't have the energy that day to try and figure it out.

"Where's Daniel, Mum?"

"He's playing in the garden," she said, as she busily fluffed up cushions that didn't need fluffing up.

"Gosh, he never seems to run out of energy does he?" I mumbled, as I turned my back to her and walked towards the garden door to watch him.

"Not like *you*, you mean?" Mum said flatly.

I stopped dead in my tracks. There were times when Mum would say something and it wasn't *what* she said but *how* she said it that got my brain ticking. This was *definitely* one of those times. The atmosphere suddenly felt uncomfortable.

"Natalie..." Mum said sternly.

Oh boy... she's calling me Natalie. She never calls me by my full first name. This must be serious.

"Yeah," I answered quietly, still with my back turned to her. I was too scared to turn around and look at her. *Then she came out with it.*

"Natalie... you're pregnant."

My heart stopped and dropped to the bottom of my stomach. I felt light headed. All of a sudden I couldn't move. I tried to but I couldn't. I heard Mum's footsteps getting closer and closer towards me until she finally stood in front of me. Her facial expression was blank. She wasn't expecting an answer, just a response, because she hadn't asked a question, she'd made a s*tatement*.

I attempted to respond but I didn't know what to say. I opened my mouth and tried to talk, but nothing came out. I was confused. Her bold statement took me by surprise. I tried to quickly think of something to say, but all I could do was silently question myself in the privacy of my mind.

What's she talking about? I'm not pregnant?! Am I?

"I'm not asking you, Natalie, I'm *telling you*. I'm your mother. I can tell," she said flippantly, as though she could read my thoughts.

She looked at me straight in the eye for a few seconds. I looked back at her. I still didn't know what to say and my heart was racing. She finally shook her head disappointedly, and then sighed deeply, kissed her teeth, and walked away. I was still standing in the same spot completely dumbfounded. I began to feel a mixture of fear, panic, and tearfulness rise up in me all at once. I also felt very defensive, and even my thoughts were tongue tied.

What's she talking 'bout? I'm not up the duff? Please! What's she talking about? What... just 'cause... What?!

There I stood, with *every* thought of reason racing through my mind, my heart pounding at a million beats per minute, and all the time a *knowing* feeling eating away in my soul. The possibility hadn't crossed my mind at any other time, but there was a conviction in me; a strange feeling that no amount of lying to myself could change. I'd taken no pregnancy test, but I knew it. I started thinking about my period, and I couldn't tell when last I'd had one. I'd been so busy with college and work and everything else that I hadn't thought about it. I then started to think about my extreme tiredness, and my constant spurts of nausea.

I was pregnant. I finally managed to move out of the spot I was stuck in and made it to the garden door. I looked over at Mum through the glass pane. She was talking to Daniel and hanging out some clothes to dry on the washing line. I wanted her to look at me and say something. I wanted her to shout or to scream at me, or just say something! I didn't know what to say, how to feel, or what to do, and I needed to hear from her. My mind was all over the place. I looked at my son... I stared at him... I felt similar to when I was back at Leon's house finding out that I was pregnant with Daniel. I was scared.

Daniel was still playing in the garden and when he finally stopped to take a breath, I saw that his shoe laces were undone so I walked over to him - but I was still wary of Mum. As I walked closer to him, and out of nowhere, I felt my heart plunge down to my stomach again. This time it fell faster. It fell sharper and harder. I stopped walking so suddenly that I almost fell over. Mum looked over at me and asked me if I was alright. I told her I was, but I wasn't. I was far from it, in fact. Mum had used her mother's intuition to figure out my situation but she had missed out one *major* detail. Yes, I was pregnant... but I had *no* idea who the father was.

Internal Cuts Show 11

Yes, just as you can identify a tree by its fruit, so you can identify people by their actions.

Matthew 7:20 (NLT)

I walked into the hospital. I was in the first trimester of my pregnancy. I was nervous, scared, and had Jenny walking beside me and Esther on my other side. We walked in... arms linked together... and everyone was *completely* silent.

I didn't want to be there. In fact, none of us wanted to be there but it was necessary. As I walked into the hospital I began to feel sick. Jenny found out what part of the hospital we needed to be in and Esther and I followed her lead. I couldn't speak. We arrived at the relevant part of the hospital, and as we reluctantly pushed through the heavy doors leading to the reception area, Esther and Jenny looked at me awkwardly. I looked back at them mirroring their facial expression. None of us knew what to say. I walked hesitantly towards the nurse sitting down behind the reception desk and took a big deep breath.

I was in the hospital for several hours. The hours felt like days. I couldn't wait to get out of there and neither could Jenny or Esther. It was a horrible, scary, and emotional time. I remember thinking that this was something I'd never want to experience ever again.

A lot of people I knew said that they didn't like hospitals, and neither did I. The whole experience made me feel uncomfortable.

Finally, after what seemed like forever, it was time to leave. As I proceeded to walk towards the exit doors of the hospital, I was numb.

I walked out of the hospital. I was still in the first trimester of my pregnancy. I was upset and scared and had Jenny walking beside me, and

Esther on my other side. We walked through the exit doors... arms linked together... and everyone was completely silent. Esther finally broke the silence.

"She looks really bad, innit?"

Jenny and I stared blankly into the distance and slowly nodded in answer to Esther's question. We'd just spent the last few hours with Shivon in hospital. She was in a really bad way and we all feared the worst because she currently couldn't breathe on her own. Earlier that evening we'd gone out to a club because I wanted to drown my sorrows and forget about the mess I was in. Shivon however, had been partying literally for forty-eight hours prior to meeting up with us, which meant that she'd already been drinking, smoking, and taking drugs. Shivon usually partied hard as a general rule, but this time was different. She'd clearly outdone herself, and although this behaviour was typically like her, it wasn't like her at the same time. It was weird. We knew her very well, so when we met her at the club we knew straight away that something wasn't quite right, and had tried to find out exactly what she'd been doing and taking for the last two days. Unfortunately, we couldn't get any concrete or straight answer from Shivon.

By the time we were fully in the swing of things and were raving into the early hours of the morning, Shivon was completely off her face. When she began to act really weird and it became evident that she was much more spaced out than usual, we began to worry. By the time we decided to take her to a hospital, she was sweating bucket loads. Shivon ended up collapsing outside of the club, an ambulance was called, and she was taken to hospital for respiratory arrest. She also suffered a seizure.

By the time we'd made the relevant phone calls to family and friends, calmed everyone down, and left the hospital, we were in a fluster and in complete shock about the night's events. I was tired, pregnant, felt a complete mess, and was desperately worried about Shivon. We all were. Esther began to cry and continued to ask questions, frantically wanting to make sense of the situation.

"I dunno... I mean what do you think this is all about? Why does she *always* overdo it? Look at the state of her! I can't believe how bad this is, and why can't the doctors give anyone straight answers?" Esther sighed heavily and hung her head, sobbing quietly before she continued.

"What if -"

"Don't even go there," Jenny sharply interjected. "She'll be cool. She's strong and *when* she gets through this, and I mean *when*, hopefully this will be the kick up the bum she needs to sort herself out 'cause she can't go on like this. I dunno what's going on with her though, for real."

"We *all* know what this is about you lot, so let's not pretend," I said harshly, angered by my friends naivety.

Jenny and Esther remained quiet while I reminded them that Shivon had recently found out some information about her estranged family, and this had brought back a lot of negative memories for her. She was *clearly* not dealing with it very well.

Shivon's mum abandoned her when she was a baby, as she wasn't in a fit state to look after her at the time, so Shivon grew up being bounced from pillar to post. Shivon was never reunited with her mum or ever had much of a relationship with her. It was common knowledge that her mum was a diagnosed alcoholic and also had some mental health issues. In true Shivon style, she would forever try to casually fob the subject off, but we knew it hurt her and the more she tried to deny it, the more she partied, the more men she met, and the more drugs she took. We always feared that she'd physically end up in a bad way because of her lifestyle, but when it happened we wasn't prepared for it.

I felt quite guilty at the time because I was the one who wanted to go out that night. I was overwhelmed with my problems and wanted to get my mind off of them. I couldn't help thinking that if I hadn't made the suggestion to go out that evening, Shivon wouldn't have ended up in hospital. Thankfully, I've realised that wasn't the truth. The fact was that Shivon had a habit, and she had done for *years*. She totally disagreed, of course. Sadly, I believe that what happened to her was *bound* to happen at some stage. I'm just glad that we were with her when it did.

Shivon was wounded, and I'm not just talking about in the physical sense. She was in pain, and had been since we met when we were seven years old. Shivon was hiding behind her masks as we all were. The only difference was that, some of Shivon's "cakes" and masks just happened to be things that could end up seriously damaging her health, or even worse, and *that's* why she ended up in hospital.

Esther and I decided to sleep at Jenny's house after we left the hospital because none of us wanted to be on our own. Jenny's parents were away for their anniversary, and Joel was hardly ever in, so we hoped that he wouldn't be hanging around trying to listen to our conversations. When we arrived, we got ready for bed but unsurprisingly, none of us could sleep. We stayed up for hours, reflecting on all of the madness that was going on. Shivon was in hospital, I was pregnant and had no idea if the baby was Leon's or Kyle's, Jenny and Gavin's relationship was hanging on by a thread, and Esther was having serious family problems. We talked for ages and got quite emotional from time to time. I had no idea what I was going to do and tried hard to detach myself from any emotion that was going on inside of me. No matter how much I tried to paint a pretty picture in my mind, I just knew that the ending to this chapter of my life would not be a good one. Whatever decision I made was not going to be an easy one either. I felt torn and I was scared.

As we continued to talk and attempt to advise each other, I suddenly had an overwhelming feeling of hopelessness. All the talking in the world couldn't fix our situations because when all the talking stopped, I would *still* be pregnant, Jenny would *still* be upset with Gavin, Esther's family would *still* be at war, and Shivon would *still* be in hospital. There we were yet again in the middle of another crisis, knowing that nothing seemed to really help or heal. Nothing brought an authentic or fulfilling sense of peace. I remember feeling verbally exhausted that evening, because there was so much talk about the problems, but no talk about the *real* solution - simply because none of us knew what it was. So as usual, we would talk... and then sigh... then maybe talk a bit more... and then either change the subject or just stop talking.

A mixture of different feelings and thoughts come to me as I reflect on this. The main feeling is thankfulness in realising and knowing what the solution is, even though I didn't know all those years ago. The solution is Jesus Christ. I can't say it any simpler. He is our restorer, our healer, and our hope. Unfortunately, before knowing and experiencing this, the name *Jesus Christ* was simply just that to me... a name.

Besides Nenna mentioning him a lot when I was a child, everything else I'd heard about Him was misinformation and a mixture of positive and negative opinions. To be honest, it also sounded a bit vague and farfetched to me at times. But in hindsight, I realise that although I'd *heard* a lot about Him, I didn't actually *know* Him, and there's a *massive* difference between the two. Not knowing Him for myself meant that when times of trouble or difficulty came, hopelessness was inevitable. This would 'cause me to lean on whatever crutch I could find, as a way to help me get through whatever I was experiencing at the time. What I could experience with my natural senses, and what was tangible, became my source of survival. I subconsciously became one of many people who use the saying "seeing is believing" as a life philosophy, when in actual fact, if I were to strip that saying down, it wouldn't hold much weight in this instance. I say this as a result of asking myself how this particular saying would apply to what I was *feeling* as I sat there in Jenny's house that night, or how it applied to what Shivon had been feeling her whole life, but had tried to hide. Neither of us could physically *see* how we felt, but we knew that how we felt was real - so it's safe to say that we *believed* in how we felt.

Although people can't physically see feelings, it's important to highlight that what we *can* see is what our feelings *produce*. A person's words, actions, behaviour, and choices are the evidence of what goes on in their hearts, minds, and spirits, and *that's* what we see - not their *actual* feelings. When I think about my mind, my soul, and my spirit, it is obvious to say that they are all as real as the sun I look at every day. I believe in them and know they are real. I may not "see" them as such, but it doesn't mean they don't exist. *Just like Jesus*. I may not have known Him, I may not have seen Him, but that didn't change the fact that He exists.

Unfortunately, I hadn't realised this yet. I had no idea that I lived, moved, and had my being in Christ. All I knew was what I was experiencing. I was hurting, it seemed as though satan had the best of me, and nothing brought hope. Everything I turned to for a resolution was a poor imitation of what I really needed. My soul cried out for something real, because there had to be more to life than what I was seeing and experiencing. More to life than just going around in circles, running on a hamster's wheel, going from one drama to the next... going from one short term fix to the next. Life was a false, empty, monotonous, and isolating existence, especially after all the props I used to entertain myself had been put away. I was lost and frustrated laying there alone in Jenny's bedroom and questioning life after my long talk with the girls.

What is the point of all of this? Why am I here? Where am I going?

It shouldn't have taken me falling pregnant to begin to reflect so much, but this was only the beginning, because I was still *me*. I was still the same old Natalie with a whole bag load of issues, insecurities, fears, and deceptions eating away at me, and I continued to live that way because it I was used to it.

I woke up later on that morning feeling ridiculously nauseous. I'd also woken up a few times to vomit that morning and was feeling really weak. I knew I hadn't disturbed the girls because they were downstairs, and I'd hoped that nosey Joel was still out or had stayed at his girlfriend's house. When I checked, I saw that his car was parked outside. I assumed he was sleeping like a baby after his long night out. I got up, tiredly slid downstairs for some water, and walked through the front room towards the kitchen with my legs feeling like lead. I also felt jealousy slither through me as I watched Esther and Jenny sleep without a care in the world. Esther was laying face down on the sofa with the head scarf she'd taken out of Jenny's room sliding half way down her face. Jenny's hair was all over the place, which I knew she'd be upset about when she woke up. She had one slipper sock firmly placed on one foot, and where the other sock had disappeared to is still a mystery. Jenny was convinced that she didn't snore, yet there she was snoring away with her mouth wide open as she slept. I smiled cheekily, with my thoughts running away with me as usual.

Oh Jen... if only Gavin could see you now, ay? This is definitely a Kodak moment.

I couldn't help but laugh to myself when I looked at them both, and I shuddered at the thought of the stench that would be Jenny's breath once she woke up, but I was still jealous that they were sleeping and I wasn't.

I suddenly felt the urge to begin to feel sorry for myself and wonder how I got myself into the position I was in, but I couldn't do that because I knew exactly what got me into the position – my choices. I still wanted someone else to blame though. I felt lonely and vulnerable and although my girls were there to support me, it wasn't enough. They *thought* they understood, but I didn't agree. We all knew that in no time at all, everything would be okay with Jenny and Gavin, and Esther's family drama would soon sort itself out. But how exactly does a pregnancy sort itself out without some serious life changing decision making? Every time I weighed up my options, I became more anxious and uncertain. There was no easy way out of this one, and there was no way on earth that I could tell Leon. I didn't even want to think about what he'd do to me if he knew the truth. There was no way I was telling Mum about the dilemma either. I wanted to tell Kyle, but I was unsure of how he'd react. Kyle and I had been cool and doing our thing for a very long time by this stage, but even if I were to tell him about the pregnancy, I couldn't tell him that I wasn't sure if the baby was his or not. I was too ashamed and embarrassed.

I spent the rest of the day at Jenny's. I slept for most of the day before we went back up to the hospital to see Shivon. We'd managed to speak to her foster mum before we went, who had told us that there was little change in her condition. Everything that was going on was too much for me. I needed to scream, I needed a release, *anything* to take me away from the chaos that was happening; and I definitely needed to make a decision.

In a panic, I decided to tell Kyle about the pregnancy.

THE UNEXPECTED 12

It is better to take refuge in the LORD than to trust in people.

Psalm 118:8 (NLT)

"You want some corn' beef and rice, babes?"

I answered by shaking my head and smiling politely, as the smell of the food travelled passed my nose, making me feel nauseous and annoyed.

"But I thought you said you was hungry," Kyle asked, clearly feeling a bit offended at my refusal.

"I just don't feel that good at the moment, Kyle. I've got a headache," I lied. I got up off of Kyle's sofa and went to lay down in the bedroom.

"Seen," Kyle grunted.

It'd taken me an extra month to pluck up the courage to tell Kyle what was going on. Between mother duties, going to college and work, plus taking turns with the girls to help Shivon get back on her feet, I'd managed to push it to the back of my mind as much as I could. Kyle and I had grown very close and comfortable with each other. I would say that by the time a year or so had passed since we met, we'd both got used to the fact that our "relationship", as unhealthy as it was, suited us both. We also knew from the beginning that we weren't exclusive to each other, although we had moments when we tried to be. Plus, being Leon's "baby mother" was always going to be an issue because Kyle couldn't stand Leon. On top of this, I was fully aware of Kyle's occasional involvement with one particularly obsessive female, but I didn't care much about that because he was a relief to me when I needed him. But recently, he'd become withdrawn and increasingly distant, and I couldn't understand it.

Initially, I thought that I was just being paranoid because I had so many things going on in my life at the time; but what came to light on this particular evening proved that I was far from paranoid.

As you could imagine, the symptoms of being pregnant was coming on thick and fast, and I was finding it harder and harder to cover it up because I was constantly throwing up or not eating much. I had also begun to show. My breasts were outrageously tender, and I wanted to cry all the time.

I'd also been avoiding Leon like the plague, and all of this ducking and diving was starting to take its toll on me. Mum had finally started to talk to me like a normal human being instead of giving me funny looks and not saying whatever it was that she was thinking. As you could imagine, her words were few, and anything she *did* say was negative. She assumed the baby was Leon's and I humoured her. I was not about to reveal to my mother all the details of the ridiculous situation I was in. She'd asked me what I was going to do on several occasions, and I had yet to answer her because I had no idea. I didn't really want the baby, but as the days and weeks progressed, the more attached I became. I kept tormenting myself, wondering if the baby was a boy or girl (I'd always wanted two boys). I tried my hardest to not contemplate the idea of keeping the baby because of the constant and agonising reality that was facing me - who's the father? I therefore tried to convince myself on many occasions, that having this baby was the most foolish idea in the world. What was ironic was that if I truly felt that way, I wouldn't have been deliberating for so long. I was subconsciously waiting for something to change, for a miracle to happen, or for someone to persuade me to have this baby, because deep down I knew that having an abortion was wrong. I wanted someone to convince me that everything was going to be okay so I could latch onto their every word and make myself believe them.

"Kyle! I beg you turn the music down man!! I'm sure I told you I had a headache!" I shouted, laying on Kyle's bed with my hands behind my head, staring up at the ceiling. I wanted some silence so that I could think straight.

After a couple of seconds Kyle turned the music down, no questions asked, no jokes cracked, no anything. It *wasn't* like him. Usually he would crack a joke or compare me to his nan, or run into the room and sing into my ear just to irritate me. Being playful was just a habit of Kyle's even if he was in a bad mood, but after being alone in his room for forty-five minutes uninterrupted, I definitely knew he wasn't being himself, and as he'd been acting strange for some time now, I definitely knew that something was wrong. I spent those long forty-five minutes trying to figure out exactly what I was going to say to Kyle, and although I wanted to know what was bothering him, I also knew that if I didn't tell him I was pregnant that day, I would never pluck up the courage to do it. I couldn't take any more ducking and diving and pretending I wasn't hungry when I was around him. I'd had enough of it all, and was drained by the constant morning sickness, which seemed more to me like "all day sickness".

As I lay on the bed, all alone with my thoughts, I felt my eyes slowly fill up with tears, as fear began to take over me. I began to sob like a baby, and then I tried to calm myself down and think rationally.

Oh come on, just stop. If he sees you sobbing like this, what are you gonna say then? Pull yourself together, suck it up, and just tell him. Just breeeaathe... come on... one, two, three, breeeeaathe...

The breathing slowly... the inhaling and exhaling ... none of it worked. I couldn't get myself together. In fact, the more I tried to stop crying, the more I cried. I felt out of control and my throat hurt due to trying to cry as silently as I could when I really wanted to holler. Once again, so many diverse thoughts, contradictory emotions, and physically uncomfortable feelings raced through me all at once. I wanted to be on my own, but I wanted Kyle to embrace me at the same time. I felt sick and I was hungry, but I couldn't eat. I was all over the place.

This is sooooo annoying. Why did I do this to myself? Why, why, whyyyyyyyyyyy!

My mobile phone was flashing with Leon's number, and had been doing so continuously for the last half hour. I ignored it. Then, to no surprise, the texts began to come through thick and fast. Leon was the last person I wanted to speak to or think about, but his relentless attitude made it hard for me to block him out, which also made me angry.

Oh, so NOW you're calling me, Leon? NOW you're texting me about your son? You make me physically want to heave. Wherever you've been staying for the last week you can go back there. Does this guy think he's slick, lying to me about staying at his cousin's since coming back from holiday? Funny how that same cousin says he hasn't seen you for months. Please. I'm so tired of you and your constant nastiness.

I turned my phone off in disgust and took several deep breaths to try and regain my focus before speaking to Kyle. The breathing worked this time. I was desperate to get this weight off my chest, so I sat up straight, fixed my clothes, and got my thoughts together as I mentally charged myself up.

Come on, Nats, you can do this. At the end of the day, Kyle knows who I am to Leon, and he can't say much anyway, especially with him doing his thing with this off key gyal. Then again, maybe this might be the excuse I can use to finally get away from Leon? Okay, maybe not... Leon would go crazy! The dramas! Hmmm... but then again it's not like it wouldn't eventually blow over, and Kyle... he's... well, he loves kids. So maybe when I tell him about the baby it might change things for the better. He might actually lock this other chick off and... oh I dunno!

I stopped over analysing everything for a moment, took a deep breath, and stomped into the front room, full of adrenaline; but I was presented with a deflated looking Kyle, sitting on his sofa with his head hung down and his phone in his hand. I was a little surprised by his demeanour. His phone was on vibrate and was flashing constantly. Although his eyes were fixated on the screen of his phone, he made no attempt to answer the call.

His obsessive chick ... it's her ringing him. It's GOT to be.

I stood there and looked at Kyle for what seemed like forever. He was despondent and I had never seen him look that way before. He was fully aware that I was standing by the doorway, yet he didn't move an inch, or say anything to acknowledge the fact. Instead, he remained silent, head still hung down, and his eyes on the phone. I began to fret.

Oh my days, suppose he already knows about the baby? Nar, but he can't... but... what if that was Leon ringing? Or... oh gosh... did Leon find out?

In a panic, I decided to just say something before *he* did. I cautiously walked towards him and sat down slowly next to him. As he went to put his phone into his pocket, I noticed that it began to flash again. My eyes gazed over the screen of the phone, but I didn't get the chance to see who was calling. He was too quick.

"What's up, babe?" I asked, guardedly.

Silence.

"Kyle, you've been like this for a while and I'm a bit worried. What's wrong?"

Silence again.

I wanted to hug him, but wasn't sure what to do for the best. Would he hug me back or give me an uppercut? I couldn't tell what was going on through his mind. He'd never laid a finger on me before, but hey... I didn't know.

"Okay, Kyle, you know what babe, I need to talk to you and -"

"Narr, I need to talk to *you*, ya know, babe," Kyle cut me off before I had a chance to fully end my sentence. The butterflies in my stomach were fluttering ten to a dozen.

He turned to look at me, and although his facial expression was stern, I could sense that it was a mask to hide the wave of emotion that he was experiencing behind it because it was obvious that he was struggling behind the bravado. I didn't know what to say. The atmosphere was thick and tense as I waited for him to continue. I was intrigued, scared, and a little anxious. I just desperately wanted to release myself from what I'd been hiding, but now his actions had completely thrown me. I panicked and started to talk again.

"Kyle I -"

"Natalie, STOP man!! I'm tryna talk to you! I'm kynna stressed out right now, you get me?" Kyle snapped at me harshly.

I was stunned and finally stayed quiet. He sighed deeply before he continued in an apologetic tone. "Look, sorry. I didn't mean to go on like that, but ..." Kyle paused mid-sentence while he irritably took his vibrating phone out of his pocket and threw it down on the table, kissed his teeth, and walked off angrily into the kitchen. I followed him cautiously.

"I swear down, this chick is annoying me *differently*!" he snapped.

"Is it lil' miss fatal attraction belling down your phone like that?" I asked with watchfulness, starting to get increasingly concerned about what was going on.

"Yeah," he sighed in frustration, as he walked over to me and hugged me tightly. I didn't know if he was hugging me out of actually wanting a hug, or just wanting a distraction. I was confused but I embraced him nonetheless. At this point it was clear that whatever was going on wasn't directly to do with me, but I was still confused. Finally he began to talk.

"Nats, you know I check for you nuff, innit?" Kyle nervously mumbled. I nodded, resting my head on his chest while he leant back on the kitchen cupboard, still hugging me. He took a huge deep breath and then he dropped the bomb on me:

"She's pregnant innit. She's six months gone and you know what, I'm not feeling this but what am I supposed to do? I don't wanna be like my dad, Nats, you know this, and I don't want this yout' growing up with me in an' out of his life, so as much as you know I'm not feeling certain ways she goes on ... I'm thinking I might have to try a ting with her."

I backed off from Kyle and looked up at him, staring at him with piercing eyes to see if I could find one small indication in his facial expression to show that he was winding me up, because he just *had* to be. I waited and waited, and stared and stared. *Nothing.* As much as I wanted this to be a joke, I knew that it wasn't. I stepped further away from him and then hurried back into the front room to grab my bag and jacket. I was speechless and just wanted to leave.

"So what, you're just gonna bounce, Natalie? You just gonna leave man hanging?" Kyle said, nervously and defensively. At that point I totally lost it.

"WHAT DO YOU WANT ME TO SAY, KYLE?!" I shouted out in a rage. "So this mad gyal is up the duff and you're gonna wifey her off yeah? So what, dat's it then? I can't *believe* this ... *pregnant*, Kyle? Are you *serious*? You're the same one that's cussing her all the time, and what do you mean you don't want to be in and out of *his* life? What you already know it's a boy yeah? Is that what you're saying to me, Kyle?"

I looked at Kyle waiting for an answer. The expression on his face gave me all the answer I needed. I was fuming.

"You know what, I don't have time for this you know, Kyle. All this time has passed and what ... you couldn't say *anything*?!"

"I didn't know all this time, Nats," Kyle shouted.

"Whatever! You LIAR."

I stomped around the front room like a mad woman, trying to get my stuff together. I grabbed my jacket and frantically tugged on the arm of the jacket that was inside out. As I was trying to fix it, I was becoming increasingly frustrated. Kyle was following me, and I was trying to get away from him and avoid eye contact because I'd started to cry. He got a hold of me, but I viciously pulled away from him and stomped out of his front door, slamming it with all the strength I had on the way out.

I knew I didn't have a right to be upset with him especially due to the dynamics of our "relationship", but nevertheless, I was. If he'd told me this news and *I wasn't* pregnant, I don't think it would have affected me as badly as it did, but because I knew what was going on for me at the time, and because I felt that I needed him so much, I saw no option but to keep the pregnancy to myself. I didn't want to risk telling him and being rejected. Telling Leon was not an option, especially as I didn't even know if the baby was his, and now my situation with Kyle had drastically changed. I was devastated. I was mad at Kyle, but even more with myself.

I spent the next few days crying, smoking weed, trying to look after Daniel, and making arrangements to have an abortion.

BROKEN 13

The human spirit can endure in sickness, but a crushed spirit who can bear?

Proverbs 18:14 (NIV)

"Nats, it's time to take your next lot of pain killers..."

I could hear Jenny's voice in the background, and I saw her standing by the door of my bedroom, but I couldn't move. I couldn't even open my mouth to speak.

"Nats..."

I shut my eyes tightly, wanting to shut *everything* and *everyone* out. I crunched up in a ball under my duvet and sighed heavily. I tried to fight the tears that I could feel desperately pushing though the lids of my eyes. All I could think about was the horrible, empty, and numb feeling that was weighing me down. My heart was heavy. I shut my eyes initially, to block out the thoughts... to block out the memory of that clinical smell of the room I was previously in... to block out the faces of the staff... the patronising tone of the anaesthetist... the "Take cares" and the "How many sugars do you want?" from the staff like I'd just taken a tooth out or something. I couldn't escape from it and I couldn't get it out of my mind. I opened my eyes and felt a fountain of tears race down my cheeks.

"Natalie, come on girl. You've got to take these," Jenny persisted sympathetically, as she walked over to hug me. "It'll be okay, girl."

As Jenny held me in her arms, I burst into tears. I cried from a depth inside of me that I didn't know was there. I cried until it hurt. I'd killed my baby that day, and I couldn't deal with the pain, the guilt, the emptiness, the frustration, or the fear. No rational words of encouragement helped, and after hours of Jenny and Esther attempting to help me look on the "bright side", they finally backed down and gave me some space.

I reached over to turn off the television that Jenny had put on earlier, but not before watching an advert which caught my attention. It was an advertisement for an upcoming documentary about fatherhood. I sighed and felt an uncomfortable emotion trying to surface, so I quickly looked away from the television screen and switched it off in record time. I had enough things on my mind without having to think about my absent father as well.

The sun was shining brightly outside that day, but I doubt I would've noticed unless someone hadn't pointed it out. I didn't care. Nothing mattered to me. Every sweet thing had lost its taste, and every bright thing seemed grey. I spent hours in my room wishing I could vanish, as my mind went over the events of the day, over and over again. I'd made a wrong choice and I couldn't change it.

I cried myself to sleep and woke up a few hours later, looking dishevelled and drained. I could hear Esther and Jenny downstairs and wondered what the time was. When I drearily looked over at the clock, I saw a glass of water on my bedside table with some pain killers that the girls had left. My throat was dry, so I reached over to get the glass of water, but as I went to reach for it, I felt a viciously sharp pain in my abdomen area. I flinched and froze. It hurt so much that the pain brought tears to my eyes. I considered taking pain killers but I didn't feel like I deserved to be pain free; the guilt of my actions was overwhelming me. As the pain died down, I was able to settle down in bed again, but then an even sharper pain overtook me once more. It *hurt*. I froze again and shut my eyes as I held my breath, trying to comprehend the level of pain I was experiencing.

A million random thoughts of different things, and different people, raced through my mind at once, and I entertained every one of them in order to take my focus off of the pain. Unfortunately and unexpectedly, one *particular* face kept popping up sporadically, interrupting my thoughts. A face that I didn't gladly welcome. A face that I hadn't pictured for years, or *ever* wanted to picture again. Initially, I couldn't figure it out and wondered why that particular person had popped into my mind at that specific moment in time; but then the penny dropped as I realised that the pain I was experiencing felt familiar... but for *very* different reasons.

In a split second my memory took me back in time to being a nine year old girl. I was cold and I was scared, as I lay down curled up on my grandparent's bathroom floor feeling pains that a nine year old child should never have to experience. I remembered repeating the same behaviour; squeezing my eyes tightly, trying to block out thoughts, and wanting to disappear - just as I was doing at that present moment in time as an adult; the only difference being that *this* time, my pain and heartbreak was a result of my own actions and choices. The nine year old Natalie on her grandparent's bathroom floor huddled up in pain, was a result of being raped. She lay there squeezing herself tightly, as if to hold onto what had already been taken from her; but she couldn't. She lay there frightened, violated, and confused.

Remembering this felt like more than just a memory, it was as though I was re-living it again. As I lay on my bed holding my stomach, eyes shut tight, I couldn't even differentiate between being Natalie the adult, or Natalie the little girl, because I felt no difference. In that moment, I was still a scared little girl lying on that bathroom floor. Maybe I'd never left that spot on the bathroom floor. Maybe I'd mentally been stuck there all my life.

It hurts... owww...

I could smell him. I could smell the scent of that man all over my body, completely invading every ounce of my personal space. I could still feel him. I could also feel the yearning for my absent father to miraculously come and rescue me and make it better... to make *me* better... but he never came. I could feel the emptiness... the never ending pit of emptiness in the bottom of my soul, screaming out, pulling me, wanting to take me in, because a massive part of my being had just been snatched away from me. This time... on this day... it was my baby that had been taken away... but back then... it was my innocence.

Nothing appeared to be different, but how could that be? Had time stood still? I felt like that same little girl who trusted in someone who chose to hurt her, let her down, and betray her trust. I hated myself for a while as I lay there confused with my past and present marrying together at the same time. All awareness of anyone else being in the same house as me escaped my mind because I felt so alone. The despair that I felt was one in which I'd only experienced in secret. No one really understood how I felt, or understood *me*. How could they? I'd never contemplated on letting anyone into my secret about the so-called friend of the family who took his "friendliness" to a completely inappropriate level with me, and I had no intention of doing so either.

And the *pain*. This awful abdominal pain kept on gripping me, but it wasn't a touch on the pain I was carrying in my heart.

"This really hurts..." I said, sobbing uncontrollably. I hadn't realised that my thoughts had become words that had actually come out of my mouth.

"Well take these, girl! Come on, I'm not leaving until you take them!"

Unbeknown to me, Jenny had walked into the room with a concerned look on her face. Esther was standing by the door holding a plate of food. Her eyes were filled up with tears, and she looked worried.

Uh oh... what exactly did I say? What did they hear?

I abruptly sat up looking disorientated and gathered my bearings, with tear stained skin and red puffy eyes. I looked around quickly, trying to pull myself together before they considered calling the men in white suits to cart me off to the funny farm. I also couldn't help but wonder how long they'd been standing there watching me; listening to me. For a brief moment I wondered if I'd let the cat out of the bag without realising, but I was just being paranoid. I was all over the place and clearly needed to get my head together.

Jenny would not relent. She gently lifted my chin and put two tablets into my mouth. She picked up the glass of water and put it to my mouth, beckoning me to drink. I looked at her reluctantly.

"I mean it... you *need* to take these. You're in here crying about the pain you're in, and we don't understand... we don't know what to do anymore... you're worrying us, Nats. You can't do this to yourself. Why are you making yourself suffer*? Come on,* Natalie... come on girl," Jenny said, slowly and softly. She looked at me straight in the eyes before continuing, and I looked back, trying not to cry.

"I'm staying here to make sure you swallow them, okay?"
I swallowed the tablets to get her off of my back. She looked relieved.

"They'll take the pain away," Jenny said with a smile. I awkwardly smiled back at her, loving her for being my friend, but ignoring the irony of her comment.

They'll take the pain away. Really? If only Jen... If only...

YOUR WAY OR MINE?   14

Am I now trying to win the approval of human beings, or of God? Or am I trying to please people? If I were still trying to please people, I would not be a servant of Christ.

Galatians 1:10 (NIV)

After the abortion things were challenging. The stress and impact of everything that happened led me into a really discouraging season. Unfortunately, the constant time off that I'd taken from work caused me to lose my job. I also fell behind on my coursework and ended up dropping out of college. Mum was being extra nice to me following an argument we had over the abortion. During the argument, she lashed out at me and made some shockingly painful and unnecessary comments. Regrettably, she wasn't the type to apologise easily; so to avoid facing the issue head on she would try to *do* things to make up for it instead. It soon became clear to me just how guilty she felt when she surprised me with an unexpected monetary gift towards my week away with the girls.

Everyone had been relatively preoccupied and distant. We had numerous things going on in our individual lives that were taking their toll on us, so we decided to get away for the week to Devon for a change of scenery. Jenny suggested it following constant arguments with Joel which was causing a lot of tension in her household, plus she'd split up with Gavin for the billionth time. Esther was meant to come on the trip, but another family issue came up so she decided to stay at home (even though Mark had offered to keep Justin and adjust his work schedule to give her a break). To take the pressure off, I decided to take Justin off their hands and brought Daniel with me as well.

The weather was warm all week in Devon, and it wasn't as busy at we'd anticipated, which made the time spent there more enjoyable and relaxing. The kids had tons of fun and thankfully, so did we. Shivon spent a lot of time resting and was finally back on her feet after a long recovery period, but we were still keeping a close eye on her. We had just come back from Devon and had dropped the children to my mum's house for a few hours so we could check up on Esther.

On arrival, Mark was leaving the house. He looked stressed out, and desperately relieved to see us.

"What's going on, Mark? Where's Ess? She okay?" we asked in unison.

"Yeah, you cool ladies? I'm glad to see you lot, still. It's been a bit nuts 'cause she's been on a bit of a mad one with her dad. You lot need to chat to her for me, 'cause I can't get through to her when she's like this. You know how she gets."

Yes, we knew *exactly* how she got. We walked through the front door and heard the banging of cupboard doors, and the clattering of pots and pans coming from the kitchen. Esther was cooking, even though her and Mark had already eaten.

"That's cool, Mark, we got this man," Shivon confidently said. Mark said his goodbyes, went back into the kitchen to grab his phone that he'd forgotten, and gave a very distracted Esther a kiss on her cheek before leaving. Mark was really attentive to Esther but it was always hard to get through to her when she was having issues with her family.

Esther was despondent and dismissive, and was rushing around the kitchen cooking up a storm. After greeting each other and calling Mum to check up on the children, we dragged Esther out of the kitchen and into the front room to find out what was going on. She was reluctant to go into detail at first. Then she finally began to explain that she'd had yet *another* argument with her dad over her leaving university and pursuing her dream of becoming a chef. Unsurprisingly, her dad was not keen on the idea, as he didn't think it was a good enough profession for *his* daughter. This had been an ongoing debate between Esther and her family, but only recently had things begun to get heated because Esther had finally decided to commit to standing up for what she wanted to do with her life.

Esther had always felt torn because of the pressures which came from her culture and upbringing, and was concerned about being disrespectful to her parents or making them unhappy. Consequently, Esther began to re-alise that the more she strived to please her parents, the unhappier it was making *her*.

"I've given up trying to explain to them," Esther said wearily. "I tried to do this uni thing, but it was only to make them happy, and I blatantly wasn't satisfied doing it anymore. I was working my socks off to get into a profession that I'm not even interested in! What's the point?"

"Esther, just forget your dad man," Shivon blurted out. "It's *your* life, not his! What's he on? Trying to make you feel bad and that? If that was me I would tell him to get stuffed, mate!"

At that point Jenny and I looked at each other and shook our heads at Shivon's ignorance.

"Don't listen to her, Ess," I said. "Shivon clearly hasn't fully recovered properly for *ever* thinking that anyone could tell *your* dad, of all people, them sort of things and still live to tell the tale." I looked at Shivon, con-vinced that she had completely lost her mind. Esther's dad was a man who held dear to his values and was not to be played with.

Everyone had a little giggle at the thought, including Esther, but the giggling was short-lived because we could see how upset Esther really was behind the laughter. She was slumped down on the arm of her sofa, looking defeated. No one really knew what to say to her.

"What's that smell?!" Jenny asked in a panic. In a split second Esther jumped up like a crazy woman, as she remembered that one of the pots on the cooker was still on a high fire.

"The rice!!" she shrieked, as she ran into the kitchen and dived over to the cooker with the rest of us in fast pursuit. She took the pot off the fire, and tried to salvage what was left of the burned rice, but it was a task she was never going to successfully achieve.

Esther slammed down the pot, threw the dish towel in frustration, and started to cry.

"Ess, its cool girl. Don't cry... it's only *rice*. Plus, at least you never used the Tilda rice... you know that rice cost papers," Shivon said, as a weak attempt to try and comfort Esther.

"Shivon, shut up man; you're getting on my nerves!" Esther yelled, while sobbing at the same time.

"I'm just saying innit... sorry, girl," Shivon said apologetically, as she walked over to Esther and gave her a hug. When she did, Esther broke down, at which point Jenny and I joined them both in a group hug. It was never easy when any of us were having a hard time, but with Esther, it was different. She wasn't as thick skinned as the rest of us, so when she cried, none of us could handle it and we just wanted to smother her.

We brought her back into the front room, this time carefully checking that all the fires on the cooker had been turned off. Esther was still sobbing away, trying to stop, but not being able to. Finally, she managed to speak.

"I just... wanted to... to *fix* it. I just wanted to... umm... make it better," she tearfully and inarticulately blubbered.

"Make *what* better?" Jenny asked cautiously, not wanting to make the same mistake Shivon had made and get her head bitten off.

"I was cooking some food to bring over to my dad. I just wanted to make it better," Esther said, sitting up straight, trying to get herself together.

"But, Ess, look girl, you know how your dad is and I know it's hard, but I think we all know it's gonna take more than a meal to change his mind about what he thinks. I appreciate how it goes with family, but maybe you're gonna have to stick this one out because it's obvious you weren't happy doing the law thing. I know your dad's not easy, but he'll come round; just like he did when you had Justin. It took time, but it worked out in the end, innit?"

Jenny's words seemed to penetrate Esther's heart and calmed her down. She remained quiet for a while.

After getting Esther to put her feet up and relax for a while, Shivon suggested that the rest of us should tidy up the kitchen. We looked at her in absolute shock. In the silence that came crashing down that second, you could have heard a pin drop.

"*What?*" Shivon asked, looking confused. "Why are you lot looking at me like that for? Don't I wash dishes, narr?"

That was just the cue we needed to burst into uncontrollable fits of laughter as we held our bellies and tried to catch out breath. Shivon was definitely not the most domesticated type, and for a few moments we wondered whether she had bumped her head while we were in Devon, or if she was on drugs again.

"You lot are bang out of order!"

Shivon was the only one who didn't find anything amusing. She jumped off of the sofa, straight faced, and marched into the kitchen, grabbing Esther's washing up gloves out of her hands.

That was the second cue for our next round of laughter. After we finished amusing ourselves, Esther had perked up slightly, and Jenny and I went to join Shivon in the kitchen. It was a breath of fresh air seeing Shivon like this. She'd calmed down massively since coming out of hospital and had apparently been doing some thinking in regards to getting in touch with some of her estranged family members. We had our reservations about it, but we decided to support whatever she wanted to do.

We had a laugh as we cleared up the kitchen, reminiscing on the fun we had and the jokes we caught in Devon. We blasted loud music in the kitchen to motivate us, and stopped our domestic duties every once in a while to have a little dance and act silly. Esther even came in to join us every now and then. As you could imagine, I was in my element when the music came on. No matter how down I was feeling, dancing always seemed to make me feel alive. I could go on and on for ages. It was refreshing to take my mind off the madness from the previous several months and dance away in my friend's kitchen, much to everyone else's amusement. In the midst of our fun and antics I couldn't help but think about how much I missed college; Shivon had been bugging me about going back throughout our time in Devon, but I really didn't feel up to going back at that time. It was sad... Shivon believed in me so much, but she never seemed to be able to see any potential in herself.

When we'd finished our jovial antics, we sat down and put our feet up, and Esther began to open up to us some more about her family. It was common knowledge ever since school days that Esther's parents were strict, but her relationship with her dad had become even more strained after she became pregnant with Justin. Esther's dad was disappointed and thought that she'd thrown away her future. She felt a huge amount of pressure because of the history of her family. Esther's dad was cut off from his family when he got together with her mum. Sadly, his family wasn't happy with his choice of a wife for a variety of reasons (but it sounded like it was more of a cultural thing and the family never spoke about it much). Years later, her dad slowly began to rebuild a relationship with his family, but he was always made to feel like a failure in certain aspects of his life. Consequently, he was extra hard on Esther, wanting her to achieve and do the things that he never got to do. Esther's mum was very quiet and timid, which left Esther feeling undefended, as her mum habitually chose to side with her dad - even when Esther knew she didn't agree with him. When Esther got pregnant with Justin, she vividly remembered her dad screaming at her saying, "It's a mess, Esther!! How are you going to fix this? This is something that can never *ever* be fixed". *Those words planted a seed.*

Esther loved her dad immensely and had never forgotten those words or the disappointment and heartbreak in his eyes, and knew that her relationship with her dad had changed for the worse that day. I've always believed that this is the reason why Esther thought she could always "fix" things and make everything better; by doing the one thing she was good at and enjoyed the most... cooking a meal.

Later that evening at home I put Daniel to bed and Leon came to visit. I hadn't spoken to Kyle, and Leon had been trying to be nice to me but I'd become distant. I still had feelings for him at the time, but I'd become increasingly tired of our same old cycles. I knew the cheating signs like the back of my hand and it was painfully obvious that he was at it again. I'd been forcing myself to sleep with him, and sometimes at night I would just look at him when he was sleeping and feel overcome with disgust because I couldn't understand *why* I was putting myself through it. I'd done the same thing this particular night and couldn't sleep, so I went to make myself a hot drink and chilled out for a while on my own in the front room. Before I drank my drink, I went to Daniel's room to check on him. I looked at my son and sighed.

You deserve so much better than this, Dandans. Mummy's trying...

The loud chant of my ring tone made me jump and interrupted my train of thought. I quickly shut the door so that Daniel wouldn't wake up, and hurried to the front room to answer the phone, hitting my baby toe on the way and shouting out in pain, while at the same time wondering who could be calling so late. It was Mum.

Ouch man! My toe is throbbing differently! If it was ANYONE else calling me besides YOU, Mum, they would've GOT IT!

When I answered the phone, although I was agitated because of my toe, I knew something was wrong. Mum told me that she'd received a call from Sarah (my old friend and the granddaughter of Sister Stewart). She began talking about Sister Stewart and suddenly my mind drifted off and I couldn't hear her words. All I could think about was the last time I saw her with her cute smile and thick glasses. As I stopped reminiscing, I heard the words from Mum that I *knew* were coming. Before I had a chance to respond, Leon had barged into the front room.

"Who you talking to, babes?"

"It's Mum, Leon," I said, shooing him away with my hands irritably. Mum was crying and this was no time to be having two separate conversations at the same time. I spoke with Mum for several more minutes before arranging to go and see her the following morning. When the conversation ended, Leon who was now wide awake, continued with his questions.

"What's going on, Leelee, is your mum cool?"

"Narr, she aint you know. You remember Sister Stewart innit?" I asked, feeling slightly lost while still trying to digest everything that was going on. Leon looked a bit confused.

"Is that the one whose grandson I used to par with in primary school?"

"No Leon, man!" I snapped.

"Oh yeah, it's the woman who's always giving them leaflet things out. That's your mum's sort of aunty innit?"

"Yeah... Well anyway, she's dead."

THE IRREFUTABLE TRUTH   15

In the beginning was the Word, and the Word was with God, and the Word was God... The Word became flesh and made His dwelling among us.

John 1:1 and 14 (NIV)

So there are three witnesses in heaven: the Father, the Word and the Holy Spirit, and these three are One.

1 John 5:7 (AMP)

*There is **one** Lord, **one** faith, **one** baptism, and **one** God and Father, who is over all and in all and living through all.*

Ephesians 4:5-6 (NLT) (emphasis added)

Sister Stewart's funeral was totally packed with people. I've never been to a church before that had people standing up at the back and flowing into the aisles. As I looked around the church, and gazed at the variety of different people inside, I wondered how such a humble and quiet old lady managed to impact so many different people's lives. I had no idea that she knew so many people. The wave of varying emotions that saturated the church made it evident to me that she was a special woman; a lot more than I'd given her credit for. People cried, and people laughed and smiled, as tributes in every style was given to the lady with a moustache who I once used to think was a little bit strange. Yet, there I was sitting in a church, overcrowded with people who thought that

Sister Stewart was definitely more than simply a "strange old lady".

My phone was on vibrate and I suddenly felt it buzzing away in my pocket. I took out the phone to see who it was, and it was Leon. Mum gave me a look which basically said "Don't even think about answering that phone in here" so I went to the toilet to see what Leon wanted, feeling slightly offended that Mum would ever think that she raised a young woman with no sense or respect.

Leon called me to argue because apparently a few nights before, I was spotted speaking to some guy he disliked, not too far away from where one of his friends lived. He was cursing and shouting, and I couldn't believe his level of inconsideration because he knew full well that I was at the funeral. As he relentlessly continued to shout at me, I chose to remain quiet and keep my thoughts to myself.

I seriously don't have the energy for this today.

When Leon finally decided to take a second to breathe, after spewing out his words faster than the speed of sound, I had only one thing to ask him.

"You finished now, Leon?" I asked sarcastically. Before he had the chance to respond, I hung up.

I looked in the mirror and began to think about everything; the abortion, Kyle, Shivon and the drugs, Esther, Jenny, Mum, Daniel, and dropping out of college. I felt so tired. I needed a change and felt empty. Earlier on in the service, the pastor had vaguely mentioned something about the magnitude of Jesus' love. I stood there seriously doubting any love that Jesus could possibly have for *me* - especially after my actions.

Lost in thought, a toilet door opened that I didn't hear or pay much attention to. I decided to wash my hands quickly and get back to Mum, and while I was frantically rubbing my hands together under the hand dryer I felt a hard tap on my shoulder.

I was startled, and as I looked up at the mirror, I saw a very familiar face looking back at me.

"Sarah?!"

"Natalie!!" Sarah screamed, as she threw her arms around me. "Oh my days, you look *exactly* the same!"

"Well I was gonna say the same thing, Sarah. How've you been? It's so good to see you. It's just a shame it had to be under these sort of circumstances, innit? I'm sorry about your nan," I said, still trying to take in how overwhelmed I felt to see her and wondering why I said *"I'm sorry about your nan"*. That phrase annoyed me.

Why am I sorry? Was it my fault? I'm sad to "hear" about her death, but to say "sorry" sounds weird to me.

"Narr that's cool, Natalie," Sarah said quickly, causing me to snap out of thought. "I'm gonna miss Nan, but to be honest I'm just glad that she's not in any discomfort anymore. I'll see her again anyway, so that's something to be happy about."

Sarah was extremely confident about her last statement and I wondered how she was able to be so confident about seeing her nan again. I was intrigued. I knew I didn't share the same confidence and hadn't ever really given much thought to what happens to people after they die. Admittedly, they'd been some really dark times in my life which made me wish that I could just disappear off the face of the earth, but I hadn't ever considered what the real implications of dying were. It got me thinking a bit, but in that moment I was mainly focussed on Sarah and how refreshing it was to see her.

"Hold on a second please, Natalie," Sarah said, as she finally answered her phone which had been ringing quietly since we first began to speak.

"Hello? Sorry, babe... okay so you're going to pick him up now? Okay cool, drive safely. Call me when you're on your way. Love you, and see you in a bit."

After Sarah hung up she apologised for the interruption. I wanted to be nosey and ask about her phone call but I kept quiet.

Sarah had grown to be quite tall. She still had the same cheeky smile, and just by looking at it brought me back to when we were children, making up dances and running around at the back of church, getting up to mischief. I sighed as the thoughts crossed my mind and secretly wished we could go back to those times when life didn't seem so dark and disappointing. I apologised to her for not making contact sooner and explained that life just took over. She seemed understanding. As we continued to talk we lost track of time, poorly attempting to try and catch up on all the years we'd missed out on in five minutes. We needed to get back to the service, so we vowed to finish catching up after burial.

On returning to my seat, the pastor of the church was elaborately speaking about the life of the late Earlene Stewart and it began to increase my awareness of how dedicated she was to her faith and belief in Jesus Christ. It was evident that through her faith, her character developed, which poured out onto her lifestyle and relationships with other people. I was amazed, reflective, and curious. I began to wonder what it would be like at my own funeral and doubted that I'd have such an impressive turn out of people who loved and cherished me the way these people did Sister Stewart. It was awesome, and the whole atmosphere was one that I can't say I'd ever encountered before at a funeral. It was a funeral by title but the day was more of a celebration of her life.

The pastor began delivering his message which began with him expressing how important life was. He began to talk about all the things that people see as being important, and concluded that these things weren't of much importance or value when push really came to shove. As he highlighted this fact, my mind wandered off and I began thinking about the story that was taking over the news that week concerning a well known billionaire who was found dead after suddenly killing himself. His friends and family were completely shocked and confused, and continuously stressed to the media how happy and content he was. Apparently, he'd just embarked on some new financial ventures in which he successfully profited a ridiculous amount of money, and had just recently come back from holiday with his family celebrating the fact. Everyone was bewildered and shocked at his death. It left me pondering on a few things.

So why did he kill himself then? He had everything that most people want, didn't he? The wife... the kids... the family... money... good health... the job he'd dreamed of since he was young... well boy...

CLEARLY something wasn't right.

I snapped out of my train of thought and continued to focus on the pastor's message. The more I listened to him, the more he continued to hit a lot of my nerves. I soon realised that some of the issues that he was addressing, were things I'd loosely considered over the years. He then began to speak about Jesus and His death. Now, I'd always thought of Jesus in *past* tense, especially because He died. But the pastor keenly reminded the congregation of the life changing importance of Jesus' resurrection and that although many years had passed since His crucifixion, He is very much alive, He is our Saviour, and that He was not just a "man", but is God who revealed Himself in bodily form (1 Timothy 3:16). He continued on by explaining that by believing in Jesus Christ and receiving Him into our hearts, we enter into *real* life, as we begin to find out *who* we really are and *why* we are here.

Hmmmmmm... okay... I'm listening... let me see what this dude is saying...

I began to wriggle a bit in my seat and didn't know why, but I continued to listen anyhow. I began to wonder if he was going to sound like many other people I'd briefly heard over the years (who I also used to think were crazy), because I could never make sense of what they were saying, and as a result I would switch off with disinterest; *but he didn't*. This time was different. He carefully began to explain and break down *why* Jesus had to die. As he was doing this, little things that Nenna used to say to me as a child began to come back to my remembrance. Things that I thought I'd forgotten. Although I was still a little bit confused and had a lot of questions swimming around in my head, tiny little parts of the puzzle slowly began to piece together and make some kind of sense to me. I didn't know *how*, but it just did. This was the first time that the reality of Christ had been broken down to me in a way that I'd never heard before. I'll never forget it, because although I didn't understand or fully appreciate the enormity of what was happening at the time, this moment played a very significant part in being the beginning of the rest of my life.

I had no idea that what was happening was part of God's plan for my life, which would shape it and change it forever.

As this man stood in front of a sea of people of all ages and backgrounds, he was fazed by nothing or no one. He had a little sparkle in his eye as he spoke and was unapologetically passionate about what he was sharing. He basically explained it like this:

Firstly, the problem is that we are sinful by nature. When I'm talking about sin, an example of this is the Ten Commandments which most of us know (Exodus 20), and if we are honest, can say we've been guilty of breaking at some stage in our lives (regardless of whether it was one of them or all of them). There's loads of other things that make us sinful; anywhere from our actions (e.g. lying, greed, slander), even down to our thoughts (Mark 7:20-23). Sin speaks of things that are an offense to God and against Gods nature.

Adam and Eve's act of disobedience at the beginning of the creation of the world resulted in our naturally sinful nature, as we are their off-spring. When they sinned, they became spiritually disconnected from God and eventually they died naturally. This was a direct result of their sin and disobedience. This was *not* how it was supposed to be. We were always meant to live in constant fellowship with God, free from death, sickness etc. (We are spiritual beings. God is spirit and we are created in *His* image, so fundamentally we **are** spirit, we don't *have* a spirit. That spirit is housed by a body. When God made Adam's body from the dust of the ground, He breathed into his body. Only *then* did Adam become a living being - Genesis 1:26, Genesis 2:7, Genesis 3, John 4:24).

Although the fall of mankind and the consequences of it wasn't Gods original plan, we have to remember that God has given us free will; therefore we have the ability to make choices. Adam and Eve made their choices. If you think about it, even as children we had to be taught right from wrong, because our nature is sinful from birth. How many times have you heard a little child lie or watched them sneak a little sweet in their pocket without anyone teaching them how to do it? (Psalm 51:5, Romans 7:18)

Although people sometimes say things like, "*Well, I'm a good person, I do good things all the time, and I certainly haven't done anything drastic or killed anyone,"* God says that we have ALL sinned and we all fall short of His standard (Romans 3:23), so I guess that blows that theory out of the water! As a result, we are then left with the effects and consequences of this which means that we're stuck because anyone who commits and practices sin is a slave to it (John 8:34), and on top of that, our iniquities makes a separation between us and God, and our sins hide His face from us so that He won't hear us (Isaiah 59:2). (Sin is more about the action, whereas iniquities are more about the underlying attitudes. It speaks of the perverseness and crookedness of our intentions which affect our will).

So being naturally sinful leaves us with a problem, but thankfully one with a solution – the solution is Jesus Christ. He is the one who bridges the gap that our sin created. Here it is in a nutshell: Just as one person did it wrong and got us in all this trouble with sin and death, another person did it right and got us out of it. But more than just getting us out of trouble, He got us into life! One man said no to God and put many people in the wrong; one man said yes to God and put many in the right (Romans 5:18-19).

Why Jesus though? Wasn't he just a man?

Well it was as if my thoughts were read as the pastor explained on.

No. Jesus *was* not and *is* not just a man. In Christ lives all the fullness of God in a human body (Colossians 2:9). Christ is supreme. Christ is the visible image of the invisible God. He existed before anything was created and is supreme over all creation. Everything was created through Him in heaven and earth. He made the things we can see and the things we can't see such as thrones, kingdoms, rulers, and authorities in the unseen world. Everything was created through Him and for Him. He existed be-fore anything else, and He holds all creation together. Christ is also the head of the Church, which is His body. He is the beginning, supreme over all who rise from the dead. So He is first in everything. For God in all His fullness was pleased to live in Christ, and through Him God reconciled everything to himself. He made peace with everything in heaven and on earth by means of Christ's blood on the cross (Colossians 1:15-20, John

1:1, 14).

My thoughts were initially silenced, but to my surprise, when another question raced through my mind it was answered once again:

There are so many other religions and beliefs. Why is THIS way the truth? Why not the many other ways that society tells us we can know God, and make it to heaven?

Because there is only one way, and that is through Jesus. He is the way, the truth, and the life, and no one can get to the Father but by Him (John 14:6). Jesus and the Father are one and He also made the sacrifice for all. If we don't believe that He is who He is, then we will die in our sins (John 8:24, 10:30). The reason for Jesus' sacrifice, the reason He had to die was because blood had to be shed, and without the shedding of blood there is no forgiveness (Hebrews 9: 11-22). So Christ made a single sacrifice for sins, and that was it. It was a perfect sacrifice by a perfect person to perfect some very imperfect people. The sacrifice was good for all time. God said "I will imprint My laws on their minds and inscribe them on their minds... I'll forever wipe the slate clean of their sins" (Hebrews 10:11-18). Christ took on the sins of the world, and when He died on the cross it was complete and finished (1 peter 2:24, John 19.30).

Now, the thing about the truth is that whether we choose to believe it or not, it won't stop being the truth! The more we seek it, the more God reveals it, but it's a journey... and to begin that journey is very simple: Repent (which is to change your mind) and be baptised, in the name of Jesus Christ for the forgiveness of your sins. And you will receive the gift of the Holy Spirit (Acts 2:38).

The Holy Spirit?...

God loves us so much that He didn't leave us without help. Without the existence of the Holy Spirit we would be left do things in our own strength. By doing this, we would fail miserably. After Jesus' death and resurrection and before He ascended to heaven, He told us that God the Father would leave us with a Helper - the Holy Spirit (the Spirit of Truth).

The Holy Spirit's job is to lead us into all truth, teach us, reveal the things of God to us, comfort us, and bring to our remembrance things that Jesus has told us. God's Spirit also gives us power (ability, efficiency, and might) and comes to our aid and bears us up in our weaknesses, even praying on our behalf when we don't know how to pray for ourselves (John 14:26, John 16:13, Acts 1:8, Romans 8:26-27, 1 Corinthians 2:10).

God loved the world so much that He gave His one and only Son, so that everyone who believes in Him will not perish but have eternal life. God didn't send His son to judge the world, but to save the world through Him (John 3:16).

Okay... saved from what? What about all this baptism talk? Come on dude, don't keep me hanging... break this down...

And he did. We are saved from the power and penalty of sin and from spending an eternity separated from God. Baptism is mandatory and is symbolic of burial of our old lives and new life in Christ which we have because of His death and resurrection. We are able to count ourselves dead to sin and alive with Christ. (Remember what was said earlier about being a slave to sin). So as sin is no longer our master we no longer live under the requirements of the law (God's law given via Moses), instead we live under the freedom of God's grace (Romans 6:5-23).

That's not to say we ignore the Ten Commandments. God's law was given so that all people could see how sinful they were. But as people sinned more and more, God's grace became even more abundant (Romans 5:20). When it's sin versus grace, grace wins hands down. God's grace is divine and undeserved favour, and it also enables us to serve God acceptably (1 Corinthians 15:10, Hebrews 12:28).

Oh wow... and there was me thinking that "Grace" was nothing more than just a girl's name and something that sounded cute...

Also, we are saved by grace through faith and not by our own efforts; therefore we can't boast (Ephesians 2:8-9). It is the gift of God. We couldn't earn it even if we tried. In saying all of this though, we are not to think that we can simply go on sinning deliberately, treating Christ's sacrifice as a common thing because there are heavy consequences for this type of thing (Hebrews 10: 26-29).

We must be born again or we will never ever see (know, be acquainted with, and experience) the kingdom of God. This doesn't mean being born again literally as in, from our mother's womb again! But Jesus says: "No one can enter the Kingdom of God without being born of water and the Spirit. Humans can reproduce only human life, but the Holy Spirit gives birth to spiritual life. So don't be surprised when I say, 'You must be born again.' The wind blows wherever it wants. Just as you can hear the wind but can't tell where it comes from or where it is going, so you can't explain how people are born of the Spirit" (John 3:3-8).

By the time the pastor was wrapping up his message, my conclusions were roughly jotted down in the notes section of my phone, which I tidied up on my second trip to the toilet:

1. Jesus is God
2. After repentance and asking God to be Master of my life, I then can go on to be baptised in water and in spirit and begin to truly live in Christ, which is a continuous journey. It's spiritual growth.
3. God's Spirit would be there to help me, and God understands my weaknesses.
4. I would be a new creation in Him.
5. The kingdom of God is within me. It's not something I can physically see (Luke 17:20-21).
6. satan is real (he's not some dude in a red suit with a fork!)

On that last point, the pastor made it very clear that the devil (satan) is very real, and that he has successfully deceived the minds of unbelievers so that they can't see the truth about Jesus Christ and how believing in Him is the light of the Gospel (2 Corinthians 4:4). Furthermore, that satan is out to kill us, steal from us, and destroy us, but Jesus came to give us an abundant life and to live it to the full (John 10:10). So there really is no grey area. Either we are living God's way or satan's way. I began to realise more and more as the pastor spoke that each and every person is an active participant in this - whether they are aware of it or not, and whether they believe or not.

The day's events left me thinking a lot about the misconceptions that I'd always had about Christianity, and I found out for the first time that I didn't have to be "perfect" coming to God because that could never be, and that it was people *just* like me – undoubtedly imperfect, that Jesus actually loves and came to save and change (Isaiah 61). I'd always thought that people had to have it all together to pursue a relationship with God. I remember on one occasion where the girlies and I had spoken on this subject after real and deep reflection on our lives. Somehow this "be perfect first" theory was what we'd always concluded, and so we figured that if this was the case then living for God was just long winded; surely it would be a waste of time even trying. *We were so wrong*. With God's grace and with the help of the Holy Spirit we could do it (Philippians 4:13). I wasn't even sure at that point if the Christian life was for me because I envisioned it to be quite boring, but all I could do at that moment was stop fighting it and accept the reassuring peace that I had in my heart, irrespective of the doubts and questions. I was completely taken aback, as I sat there feeling as though something had switched on inside of me. There was a strange atmosphere in the whole building, and I felt myself feeling a conviction inside of me that I'd never experienced before. It wasn't emotionalism, it was something deeper. Something I tried for a long time to ignore and fob off, but couldn't. Emotions change like the weather, so if it was emotions, I would've felt differently by the time I got home... or by the next day... or after the next rave... but I didn't. This stuck with me and I pondered on it for weeks.

Sarah and I did manage to catch up later on that day and we also arranged to meet up soon after. I spent that night at Mum's house, and as I lay in bed with Daniel next to me, I couldn't get the day's events out of my head. I was thinking about so many things, my mind was all over the place. I began to think about Nenna and how much I missed her. I began to think about the millions of times she'd spoken about this Jesus, and how happy and peaceful she always seemed. I thought about all the other things I'd heard, and about the other people I knew who professed to know Jesus, but didn't have the same character as Nenna or Sister Stewart. In fact, they were a far cry from being even remotely pleasant (like the people Mum disliked from Nenna's old church), and I wondered what the difference was.

Over the next few days and weeks I began to consider what the pastor had said about God giving us free will. I began to conclude that *choice* must have a fair bit to do with it. Was this part of the reason why some people didn't *look* like the Christ they professed to know and follow? Were they not *choosing* to live for God the way they should? Was their freedom of choice a massive element? Were they just not committed to Him enough, perhaps? Were they not plugging into what He has freely given them through His spirit? And surely if this was the case then wasn't this problem more about *them*, and *not* about the reality of who God is?

God is God right? Regardless of whatever people choose to do or *not* do. If a sales person is not good at their job, does that have any bearing on whether the product they are trying to sell is actually a good product or not? I don't think so. Perhaps the sales person simply needs more training and definitely needs to get to know the product better! If the product is being misrepresented, I guess the only real way for the consumer to learn the truth about the product is to try it for themselves.

I knew I wasn't an expert or knew much about God or the people of God at that stage, but I sure was thinking about things so much more differently. I spent a lot of my time thinking about the whole of the pastor's message, which appeared to be permanently imprinted on my brain from that day. I reflected on when he smiled causally, sharing his hope of Sister Stewart's name being written in the book of life which the bible talks about. He mentioned that those names which are not in there would spend an eternity separate from God, and cast into a lake of fire (Revelation 20:15), and that place is what we call... Hell.

Now, I never used to like hearing about or discussing anything to do with Hell, particularly as I was growing up. I wasn't even sure if I believed in it up until this point in my life. I didn't like the thought of it, and it made me feel uncomfortable, but *this* time was somewhat different. My new found view on things were rushing around my mind releasing an intriguing, refreshing, and strangely exciting feeling and desire for truth for the first time in my life. It was like scales had been taken off my eyes.

I have to admit that I had always been one of those people who would complain and self- righteously ask why a *good* God would allow certain things to happen, or why He would send people to a place like Hell. Well, not too long after that day it became clearer to me than it had ever been before. I realised that God doesn't "send" anyone to Hell. That's not His desire (2 Peter 3:9). If we end up there it's by our *own* choosing. Hell was designed for satan and the angels who fell alongside with him (Matthew 25:41). God has made a very clear pathway for us to avoid this place, live a purposeful life, and live with Him when we pass away, through nothing but sheer love. If we seek Him, He will be found, and we can make the choice at *any* time we choose to. However, "choose" really is the key word here. On the other hand, if we *choose* to keep Him away from our hearts, minds, lives, households, schools, and society, and in exchange we include all kinds of nonsense for the sake of doing what we feel to do with a "you only live once" attitude as we flippantly make up our own rules from decade to decade, do we really have a right to wonder why the world is crazy? *Really?* Little bit cheeky I think. Surely, there must be inevitable consequences for eliminating God out of the equation.

For many nights following the funeral, before I went to sleep, I would lay awake and ponder on these things, but one particular thing was playing on my mind. The fact remains that we only live on this earth once. Although I knew that much, it had to be said that with the life we are given, we also have freedom of choice. When it's all said and done, it's what we *choose* to do with it that counts.

Hmmmmmmmm…

OMNISCIENCE 16

Remember the former things, those of long ago; I am God,
and there is no other; I am God, and there is none like me. I
make known the end from the beginning, from ancient times,
what is still to come. I say, 'My purpose will stand, and I will do
all that I please.'

Isaiah 46:9-10 (NIV)

Many of the Samaritans from that village committed them-
selves to him because of the woman's witness: "He knew all
about the things I did. He knows me inside and out!" They asked
him to stay on, so Jesus stayed two days. A lot more people en-
trusted their lives to him when they heard what he had to say.
They said to the woman, "We're no longer taking this on your
say-so. We've heard it for ourselves and know it for sure. He's
the Saviour of the world!"

John 4:39-42 (MSG)

"How many sugars, Nat?"

"Three....."

"Three Sugars?! I'm surprised you've got any teeth left. That's a disgusting amount of sugar, Sis," Sarah shouted from the kitchen. "Oh by the way, Nat, I've only got chocolate ice cream for dessert so that's gonna have to do."

"Chocolate? Narr, Sarah. If it's not vanilla, I'm not on it. You should know this!" I shouted back.

"Some things never change, ay? I'll go shop in a bit" Sarah giggled.

Sarah and I had been spending a lot of time together since Sister Stewart's funeral. It was hard to tell that so many years had passed by. Surprisingly, her personality hadn't changed much. She was still as funny and energetic as she was when we were kids. Now that she was all grown up, the only differences seemed to be her age and level of maturity, but the same old Sarah was still present. This comforted and reassured me because we'd both led *very* different lives, so initially I doubted whether we would click like we did all those years ago. I was truly thankful that the adult version of Sarah was a version that I was genuinely enjoying getting to know, and it was clear that the feeling was mutual.

A few things had definitely changed, and 2 particular things plainly stood out to me. The first was her dress sense, which was a little bit "out there". She wore a lot of retro style accessories, and to me, none of her clothes ever worked together the way I thought they should. It wasn't really my kind of thing but it really suited her because she *somehow* made it work. I respected her uniqueness and her ability to be a bit different, and it was also refreshing to see a woman *totally* comfortable in her own skin.

The second thing that had changed was that Sarah had become a Christian. She'd made the decision at sixteen but had only started to take it seriously for the last few years. When conversing with her I was pleasantly surprised and relieved by her openness with me as I wasn't totally sure what to expect. After all the things that I'd experienced, I was reluctant and hesitant to divulge into the details of my life, so initially I kept my guard up. I didn't have the time to be dealing with being judged by anyone, but it was the total opposite with Sarah. Her transparency and frankness about her own experiences and shortcomings highlighted to me even more that everyone had flaws or areas of improvement; and when Sarah passionately shared the testimony of her life with me it was very easy to see the change that God had made in her life.

Sarah was also a person who didn't mince her words. She sort of reminded me of Shivon, but obviously not in the same way. I liked it because you may not always have liked or agreed with what Sarah had to say, but she was always straight with you, so you knew where you stood with her. This rare quality made me respect her.

That evening, we'd just come back from a concert that she'd invited me to at her friend's church and the concerts theme was "Freedom". Sarah had told me about the concert at least a month prior to the event but I wasn't really too sure about it at first. It sounded a bit cheesy and not like my kind of scene but I decided to go and I was unexpectedly surprised. My pre judgements told me to expect everyone in attendance to be goofy looking and to be singing songs that would even put Shivon on her highest high to sleep; but it was completely different and exceeded anything I could've ever expected. There were a mixture of age groups but predominantly younger people, and it'd been a long time since I'd seen *any* group of people so passionate about anything worthwhile. I looked around the church and was surprised to see people who looked just like me, people who dressed similar to me, and sounded similar to me; no one was looking at me as if I was from another planet. Although I didn't understand much of what was going on initially, I felt comfortable; this was paramount to me otherwise I would've made my excuses to Sarah and walked out. I was also inspired by the people who were doing their thing behind the microphones, and found the variety of different vocal expressions of what they called "praise and worship" quite refreshing - especially as I used to have such a one-dimensional opinion about those sort of things.

On many nights, Sarah and I would stay up late talking about all sorts of topics. She'd recently begun to school me on the dynamics of praise and worship, which actually surprised me because it wasn't about a bunch of people just singing or crying and looking crazy, it was more about really connecting with God and reverencing him. It had also helped me understand the concept and theme of the concert better as well. (I also soon began to understand that worship is actually a lifestyle). The presence in the atmosphere of the church that night was strong, serene, and truly awesome. It was undeniable, and this was a presence that I had secretly begun to want more and more of in my life. It surpassed emotionalism or hype. It surpassed a good sounding voice behind the microphone, or heart-warming harmonious waves of music just making me *feel* good. I'd grown to realise that the presence of God dwelt in that atmosphere. It was the same presence that was there when Sarah prayed for me and Daniel in my flat after Leon and I had an argument one day. It was also the same presence that I'd begun to experience when I was on my own speaking to God at night when Daniel was asleep.

Sarah was part of the dance team at her church, which excited me because I totally understood her love for dance. Thankfully, I'd had the privilege of seeing her dance at the concert that evening with three of her friends and I thought it was brilliant. *Different,* but still brilliant.

"So what then, Sarah, you think I could buss some of them moves you did today then, 'cause I had no idea you could move like that?" I asked jokingly.

"Natalie, of course you could Sis. Look, if we could dance and fling up ourselves for the devil in them raves, then how much *more* so should we for God? We can dance and it's a gift. The gift is *from* God, so we should use it *for* him, you know what I mean?"

"I hear you; I guess I've never had a reason to look at it like that before."

Sarah smiled and we both had a little bit of a chuckle as we sipped on out hot drinks. We were interrupted when the doorbell rang. Sarah jumped up and went to answer the door.

"This guy is always on a long one. He was supposed to be here ages ago, but I'm so glad you're here 'cause you can *finally* get to meet him."

It was Sarah's fiancé, Dwayne. When he came into the front room, Dwayne and I simultaneously looked at each other and leant our heads to the sides, looking perplexed. Sarah looked at me and then at Dwayne, then back at me. She was as equally confused as we were.

I know this guy from somewhere… WHERE?

"Errrr… Is someone going to saaaay somethinnnnng?" The sarcastic tone of Sarah's question almost sounded like a song.

"College… Performing Arts, right? My friend was in your class?" Dwayne asked confidently as if he already knew that the answer to his question was correct.

"Yeahhhh!!" I shrieked, "You're the little show off who used to move with Richie and dem man dere innit?" At this point I *knew* it was him. I was also relieved that he wasn't some guy that I'd messed around with back in the day. Only God in heaven knew I didn't need that drama.

"Ha haa! You got jokes. Waa gwarn, Natalie?"

As we laughed, realising that we did actually know each other and in a positive way, a reassured Sarah went to get some snacks for us. Dwayne and I began to talk and catch up, reminiscing on some of the things we remembered about college. Dwayne had attended the same college as me when I first left school. We were never friends as such, but our paths crossed a lot because we had a mutual friend. He was a little show off; always in designer clothes and drawing lots of attention to himself. He was also a little bit of a ladies man and a slight trouble maker as well. I was shocked that he was Sarah's fiancé, but even more so at how he'd changed. Of course he *looked* different, but it wasn't that; his whole persona was different and I was curious to find out what happened, and how on earth he ended up with someone like Sarah.

"I don't remember seeing you at Sister Stewart's funeral," I said curiously.

"Yeah I was, but I had to duck out early to get my little brother from the airport. Plus I was doing lots of running up and down helping Sarah's family out, so I'm not surprised I didn't see you. I'm just glad that I was there for Aunty Earlene. There was *no way* I was gonna miss that."

"Oh seen."

As he explained what happened, I remember Sarah being on the phone when I saw her in the toilets at the funeral and realised that he was the person that she was speaking to. At that point, Sarah came back with the snacks and as we laughed and joked, Dwayne began to talk about how much Sister Stewart (or Aunty Earlene) meant to him, and how his first encounter with her changed his life. For the next hour that passed I was gripped as I listened to Dwayne share his testimony and also delve into one of the closest subjects to his heart - his father.

Several years prior to our conversation that evening, Dwayne was on his way to work just like any other ordinary day, considering what girl he was going to check that evening. He was travelling on the train when an old lady with a sweet smile and a little moustache, who could only be Sister Stewart, came and sat down opposite him. He described his feelings of awkwardness because for at least five minutes straight, she kept staring at him. She finally came over and sat next to him and struck up a conversation. He wasn't really interested, but he was always taught to respect his elders, so he humoured her. After making small talk for a while she asked him a very unexpected question: *"When last you see your farder?"* Dwayne, being taken aback, was unsure how to answer and wondered if this woman was a distant relative that he couldn't remember. *But she wasn't.* He was also a bit defensive because his relationship with his father was strained, so much so, that he hadn't spoken to his father in over ten years. After asking a few more questions which Dwayne was reluctant to respond to, she went on to say the *last* thing that Dwayne was expecting: *"God wants you to see him. It's been too long. Yuh' farder is sick. Very sick... and him soon might die. Young man, you need fe go an' mek peace wid him and quick... before it too late."*

Dwayne clearly thought this woman was a lunatic and politely thanked her for her advice, but was all too relieved when his stop came, and when it did, he went to work just like he would on any other day. He even told a few of his workmates about this strange woman talking madness to him on the train and they mocked her. However, the words spoken to him kept coming back to him, not only that day, but for several weeks. He resented it because it made him reflect on his relationship with his father; something that he didn't care to think about much. As a result, he tried to focus on other things. He threw himself into "making that paper" as much as he could. He tried to "rave" it out of his mind, he tried to "gym" it out of his mind, and he tried to "sex" it out of his mind, but nothing made a difference. *His father was on his mind.*

Dwayne's father was verbally and emotionally abusive to both him and his mother while he was growing up, and it left him dealing with a lot of insecurities throughout his childhood, which followed him into his teenage years and finally into manhood. When his parents divorced, his father moved to America, and although Dwayne knew exactly where his father lived, he refused to make contact.

As Dwayne reluctantly pondered heavily on Sister Stewart's words, he couldn't understand why it was affecting him as much as it was. This led to confusion and pride preventing him from speaking to anyone about it. Now, it just so happened that Dwayne had pre-booked a holiday to America with his two closest cousins, six months prior to his encounter on the train. The travel date was fast approaching, and for him, it couldn't have come at a better time. His plan was to go and relax and get this whole "father thing" off of his mind, but as he put it, "God *clearly* had other plans". While he was in America, and after a lot of soul searching, he finally decided to open up to his cousins about what was going on. Thankfully they persuaded him to take the plunge and visit his father - with no announcement. Dwayne was nervous. He knew he had to do it that way otherwise he wouldn't have done it at all. When he arrived, he was told by a relative that although his father had been ill for several months, his health had deteriorated rapidly within the last week. He was also told that someone had contacted Dwayne's mum a while back to let her know about the illness, and that his mum had informed them that Dwayne wasn't interested, but Dwayne concluded that his relative must've been mistaken.

During his short and precious time with his father, Dwayne was finally able to build some bridges with him. It enabled him to get closure on many things that had haunted him throughout his whole life. Two days before it was time for Dwayne to return to London, his father died.

Dwayne explicitly went on to reveal how his life began to change after this happened, as God began to reveal himself to him more and more, and in different ways. He tried to run away from it for a long time and struggled to come to terms with everything that was going on. He found himself being torn between many conflicting feelings and he was desperately worried about what people would think (particularly his friends), but in the end he couldn't deny the reality of Christ and how He had impacted his life. He soon found himself attending a friend's wedding - totally unaware of the fact that Sister Stewart attended the same church. When he saw her he was totally shocked but overwhelmingly compelled to tell her everything that had happened since they met. Finally, he began to let his barriers down by gradually opening up and allowing God to come into his life and heart. That was then... and he'd been committed to living for Christ ever since.

Wow... deep.

I asked him about how his mum took the news about his father and everything that happened. Dwayne explained that when he came back to London he found out that his relative was right and that his mum had been told about his father's illness, lied to his relatives, and chose to keep it from him. If God hadn't used Sister Stewart to tell him what was going on, he would never have made peace with his father.

I was speechless but I was also inspired. As he continued to talk and transparently reveal issues that God was still working out in him, I couldn't help being in awe of what I was witnessing (and I had to respect him for his honesty). Only the true and living God could have made such a change. I knew it because I remember what Dwayne was like, and looking at him was like looking at Dwayne but looking at someone else all at the same time. I was blown away, and it was a lot to digest.

The three of us hung out for a little while longer. We caught jokes, ate ice cream and then they brought me home.

The next morning I felt refreshed and upbeat and I got stuck into some spring cleaning and household chores. I think that I went slightly overboard with it all, because I fell asleep when I sat down for what was supposed to only be a few minutes break.

While I was sleeping I had a dream. I was walking down a long road which appeared to be never-ending, and I was carrying some big and heavy weights. I was tired, weighed down, and struggling to walk. In the distance I saw a man ahead of me who I didn't recognise. Still struggling with the weights, I staggered as I approached him. I couldn't see his face clearly, but I felt peace and serenity as the weights began to feel lighter the closer I got to him. There was a bright light around him and I was desperate to get close enough to touch him and see him properly. When I tried to reach out to touch him, I harshly woke up from my sleep. I had no idea what this dream meant and at first I didn't know who the man was, but I began to have a good idea who he could have been. I spent a few seconds trying to gather myself together, and all of a sudden I began to hear a voice in my head as clear as day, saying *"I will never leave you. I will never forsake you."*

I shook my head a few times as if to shake the words out of my head, but after the shaking my head like a mad woman ceased, I could still hear it as plain as day. *"I will never leave you. I will never forsake you."*

Who is that?!! And what does "forsake" mean? I don't understand that language? Is that you, God?... YOU? Speaking to ME? Narr... I don't think so.

I knew what I felt deep inside, but my mind told me that I must be imagining things. Those kind of things didn't happen to me, maybe to Dwayne, but to *me*? I kind of still struggled with the idea. The dream remained on my mind for the rest of the day. By the end of that week it was still niggling away at me. I started to feel a little bit like how I imagined Dwayne may have felt when he described not being able to shake off what Sister Stewart had said. I tried to rationalise it, telling myself that it was just a coincidence. But then I remembered how I felt at the funeral; how the pastor's words kept coming back to me and how I'd been feeling ever since. I knew something was going on, but I couldn't help questioning myself. I briefly considered asking Sarah about it to see what she thought, but I decided to keep it to myself instead.

EPIPHANY

17

... One thing I do know. I was blind but now I see!"

John 9:25 (NIV)

You intended to harm me, but God intended it for good to accomplish what is now being done.

Genesis 50:20 (NIV)

"Isn't that Alesha from your old work place, Jen?"

"Yeah, Ess, that's her," Jenny mumbled, as she re-applied her lip gloss while dancing to the music and smiling with the DJ at the same time.

"She should *never* have worn dem shoes with those corns on her toes though. Her toes are blatantly hanging over the shoes! What's she going on with?" Shivon blurted out over the loud music as she walked over to the bar.

"Shivon, *please* take it easy tonight," I pleaded.

Me and the girlies were at our usual raving spot. Many months had passed, and over those months I began to feel differently about my life. Every so often the girls tried to get me to go out, but I had drastically begun to lose interest. It wasn't the same for me anymore. I was only out on this particular night because it was Jenny's birthday and I wouldn't have heard the last of it if I didn't attend; plus I wanted to help Esther keep an eye on Shivon. It wasn't fair for Jenny to have that responsibility on her birthday, and Esther couldn't manage Shivon on her own. Unfortunately, Shivon had begun drinking and taking drugs on and off again. We were thankful that she wasn't as deeply involved in it as she was before, but due to her ending up in hospital previously, we didn't want the same thing or worse to happen again so we were trying to keep a close eye on her.

She'd briefly mentioned something about hating her family and about them being "too mix up", a few months prior when we were out shopping one day. But when we asked her to elaborate she got defensive and didn't want to talk about it. Our suspicions were that, whatever had recently taken place with her family was the reason behind her relapse. We tried *so* hard to help Shivon but she was *very* hard headed. Not even the strict warnings from her doctors were enough for her.

As the night went on, I began to feel increasingly more detached from what was going on around me. As I looked around I saw the same old thing, the same old hype, the drinking, the number exchanging, the clothes, and the whole charade. It had become so *boring, empty* and *pointless* to me. I felt like a character on a film who's standing in a crowded room with lots of things going on around them, but all the while they feel like a stranger as they stand there completely disengaged as they inwardly stand out from the rest of the oblivious crowd. I couldn't deny it; this wasn't for me anymore and I *knew* it.

I was bored of the lifestyle I'd been engaging in my whole life and my soul needed something more than what this existence appeared to offer. I spent the next few hours forcing myself to look interested in what was going on for the sake of Jenny. I also passed the time by playing around with my phone.

This is long. What am I doing here? I wanna go home.

I had at least seven missed calls from Kyle. He'd been calling me for months and I continued to ignore him. The last I'd heard, his son was walking and looked just like him. Kyle was also still messing around with his son's mum, but it was common knowledge that he was doing his thing with other people at the same time. I missed him and was still hurt about everything that happened, but I couldn't deal with the drama anymore. Leon was just about enough for me. I wanted to change my number, nevertheless, I didn't want to deal with the lecture I'd get from Leon.

A few days after our night out, I was chilling out in my pyjamas at Shivon's house with Daniel after spending the night there. Esther stayed over as well but had left to pick her mum up from her crazy early morning shift at work. We'd spent half the night trying to get Shivon to realise that her behaviour was damaging her and surprisingly she admitted that she was fully aware, but it was her way to block out her feelings. I felt upset for her. In fact, I felt upset for *all* of us. Shivon didn't know it, but I'd asked Sarah and Dwayne to keep her in their prayers even more so than me. It's not that I didn't need the prayers, but Shivon *always* worried me. She just had a knack for being reckless and mindlessly self-destructive even at the best of times.

It was ridiculously early in the morning, and none of us besides Daniel had slept. Shivon and Daniel were wide awake and energised, whereas and I was half asleep on the sofa. I jumped out of my skin when Shivon's phone began to ring, but she was too busy playing computer games with Daniel and couldn't be bothered to answer it. I had to question who the child was as they both teased each other, determined to beat each other's score.

"Aunty Shiv, you're rubbish!"

"What? Dandans, this is only the first round you know! Watch what's gonna happen to you now," Shivon said acting jovial.

The pair of them were hilarious, but it was way too early for the noise so I dragged myself off the sofa to go upstairs and rest for a while; but I noticed that Shivon's phone kept on ringing. She reluctantly put the game on pause and came over to answer it, while I half-heartedly played the game with Daniel to keep him quiet while she had her conversation.

"Jen, what's going on? You disturbed me you know love, I was... WHAT? Slow down, girl, I can't hear you!"

I was barely concentrating on the game anyway, but when I saw Shivon's facial expression my concentration was totally lost.

"Arrrr haaaaaaaaa!! Mum I beat you!!!" Daniel yelled.

"Ssshhh, Dandans, Aunty Shiv's on the phone," I said irritably as I rushed over to take the phone from Shivon. Jenny wanted to talk to me.

"Wassup, girl?" I asked hesitantly. I tried to read Shivon's facial expression as she handed over the phone to me. Her expression didn't give much away apart from the fact that something was wrong.

"Wassup with your phone, Nat's man, I been trying to get you?! It's a madness, girl, I'm coming round. Don't answer the door, girl; Leon's on his way round to you now! Joel's such a fool, he makes me sick!"

Jenny confused me because what she was saying wasn't cohesive and the fact that she was speaking so fast also didn't help.

"Jenny, CALM DOWN!" I yelled. "What's going on? I can't understand what you're talking about!"

Although I didn't understand what was going on straight away, my heart began to pound viciously once I heard her say that Leon was on his way to Shivon's.

What's going on NOW? I hope Leon isn't on a hype 'cause I'm just not in the mood for it. Lord help me!

Once I managed to calm Jenny down, she prudently explained that during a party that had not too long finished, Leon and Joel (as in Jenny's brother) got into some kind of argument over Joel's girlfriend outside of the club. Apparently, Joel said something to Leon about me that made him really angry, and as a result he was on his way to Shivon's house as we spoke. I was scared, frustrated and in a panic. I hadn't turned my phone on since I'd woken up, and at that moment I considered turning it on to see if Leon had sent me any messages, but I was too scared. I decided to try and get a clearer picture from Jenny instead.

"Yeah I hear you, Jenny, but *why* though?" I was getting really frustrated.

"Natalie, what *exactly* is going on, man?" Shivon blurted.

"Shivon, shut up man, I can't think straight with all the noise. Turn the game down!!"

Before I had a chance to ask any more questions or check my phone due to Jenny's vague explanation, I heard the doorbell ring. I hung up the phone and then I heard it ring again, and again, followed by the person just keeping their finger on the bell. *It was Leon*. I could tell that he was mad just by the way he rang the bell. Shivon was panicked and my stomach was doing somersaults. I was petrified but I didn't want to scare Daniel. Shivon didn't know what to do; she kept looking at me, then at the front door and then back at me in a total frenzy. I told her to answer it.

"Nats, are you *crazy*? Just leave him out there!"

"Shiv, just get the DOOR!" I yelled. I knew better than anyone that Leon was *not* going to go away, and I was scared of what would happen if I called the police.

Shivon answered the door while I tried to take Daniel upstairs, but he wouldn't go with me after he heard Leon's voice. As soon as Leon stepped through the door and as soon as I saw his face, I knew it was *on*. I tried to keep Daniel as close to me as possible but with him being a total daddy's boy, it was proving difficult.

"Daddy!!" Daniel shouted

"Take my son upstairs," Leon said to Shivon bluntly.

"*Look,* Leon, I don't want any dramas in my yard you know. Think about little man! Just allow it."

Leon looked at Shivon as though he wanted to punch her lights out. He stood there silently... nose flared... and breathing heavily. Before he had the chance to tell Shivon about herself, I asked her to take Daniel upstairs. She was justifiably hesitant.

"Leon, if you lay *one* finger on her I'm calling the feds and I mean it. I don't want any drama!"

Shivon was straight-faced, as she nervously escorted Daniel to her room, along with the games console. My insides were turning, but I stood strong... scared as anything... wondering what on earth was going on.

Jenny, why wasn't you more clear!!! I have no heads up on the situation and I dunno what he's mad about.

Before I could say anything Leon blurted out, "So you aborted my yout', Natalie, yeah?"

I was stunned but remained under control, wondering how on earth he managed to find out what happened.

"What?... ARE YOU TRYNA TAKE MAN FOR SOME KIND OF FOOL

OUT HERE OR SOMETHING?!" he shouted like a mad man, hurrying towards me.

I was frozen. Fear gripped me and I couldn't move. By the time I attempted to answer his question it was... too late.

"Leon, I -"

BANG. Leon's fist struck my face. The pain was sharp and travelled at record timing up my nose, to my eyes, and then to my head. My eyes were watering heavily as I jolted backwards. I couldn't open my eyes and was dazed and stunned by the pain. I heard Leon begin to swear and shout at me, calling me every name under the sun. I was trying to answer him, but every time I tried to speak he'd hit me and stop me dead in my tracks. I started to cry, whilst at the same time trying to defend myself, but it was all happening so fast. I ended up cowering down on the floor with my arms raised upwards to defend my face. I had always tried to fight Leon back before but I was no match for him physically. I was scared of him. I tried to back away whilst being conscious of Daniel hearing too much so I tried to lower my voice, begging and whimpering, but Leon wouldn't relent. He kicked me like I was a dog as I huddled up on the floor, with him shouting and cursing venom at me at the same time. I could hear Daniel shouting something from upstairs but it was covered by Shivon violently screaming at Leon. I had no idea what was going on around me. My eyes were shut tightly, and I was in a complete state of fear, pain, and disorientation, anticipating every blow. I remember feeling someone trying to lift me up from the floor. I could hear Shivon's voice near me so I thought it was her, but when I looked up, it was Leon. He grabbed me and pulled me up by my pyjama top until I was adjacent to him. He then held me by my neck and thrust me against the wall. Shivon was trying to pull him off of me.

"Daniel!" I tried to cry out in between my tears. I was blinking a lot, trying to see where Daniel was through my tear filled eyes, but I couldn't see him. My breath was short because of the pain I felt in my torso area.

Leon put his face close up to mine as he threatened me, but I don't remember much of what he said.

Shivon was still screaming and shouting, and Leon pushed Shivon and threw me onto her sofa, promising that he wasn't finished with me and that he was coming to take his son. He finally stomped out the front door, kicking some of Shivon's furniture on his way out. Shivon ran over to me in a frenzy attempting to sit me up straight, but it hurt too much. She was crying her eyes out and repeatedly screaming, "I'm gonna kill him! I swear down I'm going to dead that brudda!"

Everything was a blur to me. I was in so much pain and it became worse every time I tried to move. Everything hurt, my ears were ringing, my head was pounding, and my body felt like I'd just been run over by a bus, yet all I wanted was my son. I finally looked up and saw Daniel at the bottom of Shivon's stairs looking straight at me, stiff as a plank of wood, and with a facial expression of such bewilderment and fear that I will never forget it. I looked over to Shivon's glass cabinet which stood at the side of where Daniel was standing and I saw my reflection. I looked a complete mess. I heard a noise at the door and jumped out of my skin because I thought it was Leon again, but it was Jenny standing in the doorway, stunned and *completely* horrified.

"Get... Dan... out of here," I said breathlessly, as Jenny detoured from coming over to me and approached Daniel instead.

"*I'll* take him!" Shivon said defiantly, looking at Jenny as though *she* was the one who just attacked me. "Look at the state of her, Jenny, what's going on man!! That brudda is gonna dead, I'm telling you!! How did he find out about the abortion?!"

Jenny raced over to me and tried to console me. She gave me something to put on my busted lip but I didn't want to be touched. I was crying, panting from the pain, and I wanted answers.

"Oh my days! Girl, I need to take you hospital!" Jenny cried.

"Did YOU tell Joel, Jen?" I tried to yell at Jenny but I was in too much discomfort. I cried instead.

"No I didn't! Awww, girl, I'm so sorry," Jenny pleaded with tear filled eyes.

I tried to avoid going to the hospital, but with the pain I was in I didn't have a choice. I also didn't know what I was going to tell the people at the hospital either.

The next few hours were a blur to me as I was taken to hospital and was asked a million and one questions about my injuries and how they occurred. It was a drama. Daniel was taken to my mum's, but once she found out what happened *another* saga began because she was on the war path and wanted Leon's head on a plate.

In the end, I found out what *really* happened: When I had an appointment for the abortion prior to the procedure, Jenny took me to the appointment in Joel's car, but I accidently left some incriminating evidence in the car... and he found it. He confronted Jenny about it, thinking it belonged to her, but she denied it and tried to style it out. Joel wouldn't relent and concluded that if it had nothing to do with Jenny, then me or Esther had to be the culprit. Throughout all of his interrogation tactics, Jenny stood her ground and told him nothing. In her defence, she did tell us about it at the time, but as Joel couldn't prove anything we left him to presume whatever he wanted and we assumed the topic was dropped. However, when I stayed at Jenny's house on the night when Shivon went into hospital, I woke up and went to the toilet to be sick several times. I thought Joel was sleeping - *but he wasn't*. With hearing me being sick, and unbeknown to us, him picking up on a few of our conversations, he put two and two together and unfortunately for me - got four. He initially decided to keep it to himself, but when he went to this party, had one too many drinks and saw Leon trying it on with his girlfriend, Joel got mad, confronted Leon, and the abortion information all came out.

With all the frenzy going on around me with people asking questions and talking and wanting Leon's head on a stick, plus people in our circle bad mouthing me, all I cared about was Daniel. I didn't care about anything else. I couldn't get his fearful facial expression when he saw me out of my head and it broke my heart.

Something in me died that day but something was also birthed because I knew without a doubt in my mind that I couldn't go on like this anymore. I was glad that I'd been asking Sarah and Dwayne to pray for me because I knew I was going to need prayer more than ever. Something had to change... and it did. But for the time being I ended up with a black eye, cracked ribs, and stitches in my lip and the back of my head with lots of bruising and other minor injuries.

It was the worst beating I'd ever got from Leon... but by the grace of God... it was also the last.

Moving Forward 18

I don't mean to say that I have already achieved these things or that I have already reached perfection. But I press on to possess that perfection for which Christ Jesus first possessed me. No, dear brothers and sisters, I have not achieved it but I focus on this one thing: Forgetting the past and looking forward to what lies ahead, I press on to reach the end of the race and receive the heavenly prize for which God, through Christ Jesus, is calling us.

Philippians 3:12-14 (NLT)

Above all, you must realize that no prophecy in Scripture ever came from the prophet's own understanding, or from human initiative. No, those prophets were moved by the Holy Spirit, and they spoke from God.

2 Peter 1:20-21(NLT)

It was early on a Friday evening. I remember it like it was just the other day. I was standing on the balcony of Jenny's tenth floor flat, staring out at the beautiful view before me. The sky was an amazing blend of yellows and oranges mixing together to produce a breath-taking view of the sun setting. I looked at the birds flying fiercely towards their destination. I was inspired by them, and could relate to them at that moment as I wondered whether they felt the same way as I did right at that second - free and liberated.

As I stood on Jenny's balcony with such an awesome view in front of me, I leant my head back and inhaled the fresh air. Unlike every other day, *this* day I decided to embrace every ounce of nature around me. I began to look beyond the hustle and bustle that was below me... to ignore the concrete jungle that had coerced me daily to never look beyond it, and instead, I looked at the world with different eyes. For the first time, I was able to *really* see the beauty of God's creation that I'd spent my whole life being surrounded by, but had never really appreciated. I turned around to see Jenny standing behind me smiling.

"You're *really* in your own world aren't you, girl?" Jenny said softly, as she came out to join me.

"The sky does look nice though, Jen, I mean... look at it. *Really* look at it. How anyone can say there's no God is beyond me."

"I hear you, girl. It's gorgeous innit? I need a holiday."

Jenny had invited me and Daniel to the flat she'd moved into shortly after the drama with Joel and Leon. Unfortunately, her relationship with Joel had plummeted into a non-existent one after Leon physically attacked me, and to add, Jenny had found herself a new boyfriend - much to Joel's disapproval. Due to all the arguments they were having in the house and the stress it was causing her parents, she decided to move out. At this point she'd been there for about a year and appeared to be much happier. In fact, she wasn't the only one who was happier... I was too. So much had happened since the Leon fiasco. It was unfortunate that it took something like that to get me to a place of serious decision making, but when I think about all the positive changes that occurred afterwards and even leading up to it, it was definitely worth everything that I'd been through up until that point (although I would *never* want to experience it again).

The whole process had taken time. During the aftermath of Leon's violent attack, I totally broke away from him for a short time but I eventually let him back in. I knew that something had to change, but at the same time I became even more scared of Leon and was at an all time low. Leon was like a dog with a bone that he wouldn't let go of and I was a total emotional mess, with not much fight left in me. He started laying on the charm and behaving in ways that I had never seen from him in all the time we'd been together. This made me feel torn between what I'd always wanted from him, and what my spirit yearned for which was God, peace of mind, and a better life.

Soon enough, Leon's behaviour began to fluctuate regularly from hot to cold. I thought I would *never* get away from him properly, but by God's grace things finally began to fall into place. Little by little, I could see God making a way in what I thought was an impossible situation. After the back and forth with Leon and feeling trapped for so long, I began to move further and further away from my old life and closer to the new life that God always had for me.

Miraculously, Leon's stalking and taunting became less frequent, and with a lot of faith, prayer, not to mention the support from my girlies and new found friends, my life began to turn around in a way that only Jesus could turn it.

As I stood on the balcony staring out as far as my eyes could see, my legs began to feel a little achy, so I went inside and grabbed for the hot drink Jenny had made for me.

"I think I've gone and overdone it today, Jen," I said, wincing in pain as I sat down.

"Yeah I can tell," Jenny giggled, along with Daniel adding his infectious laugh to the equation. "Oh well, never mind, Nats. At least when you go in tomorrow you can work off all the food I'm about to stuff you up with!"

"Yeah I guess so," I laughed.

I'd finally decided to go to back to studying and pursue my dream of doing the *one* thing that got my heart racing – dance. I decided to go all out, and I was in my first year of a doing a BPA (Hons) in Contemporary Dance, which I ended up getting onto with some serious favour from God. Due to previously dropping out of courses and being inconsistent with my studies, I shouldn't have got onto the course and I knew it. I'd spent weeks with Sarah praying about this, and God didn't just open the door, He literally flung it open and I excelled in my audition which was part of the entry requirements. Ironically, a few of my old class mates didn't get onto the course even though they actually remained in college and kept their heads in their books. I felt so blessed and undeserving of what God was doing in my life but I was totally thankful. My plan was to finish the training programme after three years and then go on to do a postgraduate programme, if God would have it that way.

After drinking my hot chocolate, me and Jenny spent the next few hours eating and slumping out on the sofa while Daniel was playing. As we giggled and chatted away, I was completely oblivious to how quickly time had passed. I hadn't seen Jenny properly for a little while up to that point, so it felt like there was so much to catch up on even though we spoke on the phone often. Everyone was so busy getting on with their lives that we hadn't really had as much girlie time as we were we used to. Esther and Shivon were also doing their thing. We hadn't grown apart as such, we were just all caught up with life. Daniel was also doing really well, but it'd taken me a long time to get his behaviour to settle down after he saw what happened with me and his dad. It was hard dealing with his school and so many things all at once. Without the support I received from friends and practical support from my mum, I wouldn't have got through it; but God was with us both and allowed the right people to be around us at the time.

"How's Joel?" I asked cautiously. Jenny didn't like to talk about him much.

"He's alive," Jenny grunted, clearly not wanting to elaborate. I ignored the hint and pursued the conversation.

"Jenny, he's your *brother*. I know he's got his ways, but don't you think it's about time you guys squash things and just try to be cool?"

"Things will *never* be cool with me and him, Nats, and you know this. Everyone knows we've been hot and cold since we were kids and that's just how it is," Jenny said dryly.

I took a deep breath before I continued.

"Jen, I of all people know how you feel about the Leon thing but that's over now, and more importantly, let's just be real and get down to the root of it as well. Don't you think it's about time you forgave him *properly* for burning your face? It's not like he attacked you is it? It was hot milk. It was an accident, and you lot were kids."

"I *do* forgive him, Nats, but he really gets under my skin! I feel like he's always in my business, just messing things up in my life and getting involved in everything. He loves to comment and pass judgement on *every* single man I meet, but he doesn't understand how hard it is just to find someone who won't find the scar a turn off. *I'm* the one that has to deal with covering it up and the messed up comments people make, not him. Plus he's got a big mouth and you of *all* people know this," Jenny said defensively.

"Yeah I *do* know this, but I-"

"Nats, I seriously don't wanna talk about that dude today, I really don't. How's Sarah?" Jenny asked, sharply changing the subject. I decided to drop the Joel thing.

"Yeah she's cool. We got dance practice this week so I dunno how that's gonna happen with how I'm feeling at the moment, but everything's gotta be on point for the conference next month. I'm well excited."

Jenny gazed at me, deep in thought, and smiled at me in the same way she had when I was on the balcony earlier. Then she sighed heavily.

"What?" I asked curiously.

"It's *you*, Nats. You're still the same, but you're so different at the same time. I never thought I'd see the day that you...YOU would get *baptised* and all that. And look at you now; you're bang on this church ting and just doing what you've got to do."

"It's not a church *ting*, Jen, how many more times, girl!" I laughed.

"Yeah, yeah, Nats, it's a 'relationship with Christ' as you keep on saying."

After a few minutes of silence Jenny leaned forward as though she was about to say something but she stopped herself. It was clear that she had something on her mind. I was going to ask her to come out with whatever it was she had to say, but I decided to wait for her to speak in her own time. Admittedly, there was a time when I'd get a little bit defensive about my new lifestyle because I knew that it surprised some people, and they couldn't understand it - especially those people closest to me. Mum definitely had a lot to say at first. On the whole, most people were cool but naturally had their opinions about it. The more time went on, the less I cared, because the things that were happening in my life were so profound and divinely appointed which subsequently gave me a new sense of boldness when dealing with people and their speculations. All I had to give was my story... and that was more than enough.

Jenny attempted to speak again but still struggled to muster up the words. After curiously watching her meditating and seemingly battling with her thoughts, she finally spoke.

"I have to admit, I'm still amazed about what that woman said to you at church that time you know. I remember when you first told me. I was thinking about it for days and days. That was deep."

I tried to remember what she was talking about because so many mind blowing things had happened over the last year, it was hard to keep count. Then I realised that there was only one thing that Jenny could be speaking about because I remember her reaction at the time.

"Yeah it was, Jen, I agree, but it was clearly part of Gods plan," I said, smiling at the memory. We then spent a little while reminiscing about what happened.

Basically, some time after I recovered fully from my physical injuries inflicted by Leon, I went to church with Sarah. Around that time I also remember getting the revelation that although bruises and physical injuries heal, the deep wounds inside need a different kind of healing. I was hurting, and the truth was that I'd been hurting for *years*. There I was, a young woman and mother responsible for a little boy, yet I still felt like a little girl inside.

The service that day was amazing and it was refreshing to be in the presence of the Lord, in His house, surrounded by people who knew and loved Him. But I sat there smiling and silently screaming inside as I pondered on the *many* causes of my internal pain (that I was aware of). I was also still worried about Leon at the time.

As I was leaving church that day, the woman who had preached (who was also a first time visitor at the church) approached me. I was taken aback at first and wondered what she could possibly have to talk to me about, but she was very pleasant and I felt comfortable enough around her so I allowed her to speak. She said that she wanted to pray with me and Daniel, so I allowed her to do it. God knew I needed all the prayers I could get. While she was praying and as I listened intently to her words, I realised that this woman somehow seemed to know *exactly* what I was feeling. She knew I was in emotional pain but even more bizarrely, she also knew particular details about my life. These were things that she couldn't possibly have known because they were things that I spoke about with God and God alone. She said things... *little* things that were so close to my heart that I became slightly scared of what else she was going to say! I didn't know what to think and initially became paranoid.

Does this woman know ALL my business? Who she been speaking to?

After she prayed, she told me that God wanted me to cast my cares and burdens onto Him because He cares for me. She began to talk to me about the rape when I was a child, and the pain I still carried regarding my father. I was perplexed as I sat there silent and stunned, with warm tears streaming down my face. How did this woman know all this? This was some random woman from Wales who had visited the church for the first time, and whom I'd *never* seen before in my whole life. No one could've told her these things because no one knew these things besides *me*. As this woman continued to speak there was such a knowing and pulling in my spirit and I knew that Jesus was with me and speaking to me through this woman, but I still struggled to comprehend this level of divinity even though I couldn't deny it. As she comforted me, she commented again on "casting my burdens", but this time referred to them as "weights". She told me to drop the weights off and give them to God because they are weighing me down; and as she spoke, the dream that I had immediately came back to my remembrance. The dream that I had told no one about began to make sense. I remained silent, but I cried. Before we departed, she gave me a huge hug and told me that the Lord told her to tell me that He will never leave me or forsake me. I was stunned. *There were those words again*.

The following morning, I woke up with an undeniable feeling inside of me that was prompting me to pick up my bible - so I did. I didn't know why, and I definitely didn't know what I was looking for, but as soon as I opened the pages and looked to the left part of the page, there it was literally screaming at me: Deuteronomy 31:6 *"Be strong and courageous. Do not be afraid or terrified because of them, for the LORD your God goes with you; He will never leave you nor forsake you"*.

I will never leave you or forsake you. There it is…

I looked up the word "forsake" and basically, God was telling me that He was with me and wouldn't abandon me. I was dumbfounded but comforted and I had an unexplainable peace, knowing that Leon wouldn't be much of a problem for much longer. I didn't know *how* it was going to happen but I just knew it. The following week a similar thing happened, only this time I was led to a scripture that I had never heard of but knew *immediately* that it was for me: Matthew 11:28 *"Come to me, all you who are weary and burdened, and I will give you rest."* I knew even more in that instance that God was talking to me, and I understood even more what the dream was about. I was overwhelmed. During the weeks to follow, God began to reveal Himself to me in so many different ways, and I knew I had to stop running away and fighting what I already had begun to know was true and fully accept Jesus Christ into my life. So I did.

Since then, I went on to be baptised and was getting support and teaching which was important as it was all *very* new to me. I was excited and was in a place of positive anticipation. In the meantime, my whole life began to do a one hundred and eighty degree turn for the better. I was studying what I loved, and found myself dancing with Sarah in a dance group she was part of. I felt so alive!! When Sarah had made that comment about "dancing for God", I have to admit that I didn't fully understand what she meant; I thought it was slightly comical and remembered having all sorts of thoughts at the time:

Dance for God? How am I supposed to shake myself up for God?

But since becoming a Christian and really learning about God's nature and his purposes and plans for us, it started to become clearer, and dancing soon began to be a different experience for me as my understanding grew. I really began to understand that my ability and love for dancing came from him. So to have the pleasure of dancing in his presence was an act and expression of worship and was also a privilege; one in which I was in awe of because dancing had a completely different meaning to me now compared to before when I was flinging up myself in the clubs and raves. I had embraced the treasure and pleasure of using my God given talent for *Him* - not for satan. What Sarah said had become something I was able to understand and experience for *myself*.

With all this said, I was definitely still a work in progress, but for the first time in my life I was actually *living* and not existing. I will also say that everything in my life from that point on wasn't perfect either because that's a common misconception. However, the truth about life became more apparent as the Holy Spirit began to teach me and open my eyes more and more to what I was previously ignorant to. Some things made me sad, like when I thought about how blinded, shallow, and deceived I was, and naturally I wanted my girlies to see what I'd begun to see. We'd spent so many years going around the same mountains and I'd finally realised that in all of the searching, Christ had always been the answer. I was desperate for them to be saved.

Thankfully, the girls were supportive and came to church with me a few times. Jenny and Esther were receptive enough and Shivon mainly came to check out the guys but, hey... at least she came. I was just thankful that she stepped foot through the church doors. I knew the Holy Spirit tugged at them at times, but I also knew that they struggled because of fear and pride. They wanted and needed change but also wanted to stay in their comfort zones, even though what they *thought* was comfort were the very same things that were entrapping them. I understood fully because that was the place where I was only just coming out from. All I could do was keep it moving with God and actively love and encourage them whilst continuing to pray, with the hopes that God would continue to water the seeds that I knew had already been sown in their hearts.

I left Jenny's flat that evening and went to bed reflecting on everything that we discussed. I was so thankful to God that I was now at a place where I could look forward to my days ahead instead of secretly hoping they would swallow me up.

The days turned into weeks, and the weeks into months, and the months into years, and as time went by I continued to walk with the Lord... and I never looked back.

THE REMEDY 19

And a woman who had suffered from a flow of blood for twelve years and had spent all her living upon physicians, and could not be healed by anyone, came up behind Him and touched the fringe of His garment, and immediately her flow of blood ceased. And Jesus said, Who is it who touched Me? When all were denying it, Peter and those who were with Him said, Master, the multitudes surround You and press You on every side! But Jesus said, Someone did touch Me; for I perceived that [healing] power has gone forth from Me. And when the woman saw that she had not escaped notice, she came up trembling, and, falling down before Him, she declared in the presence of all the people for what reason she had touched Him and how she had been instantly cured. And He said to her, Daughter, your faith (your confidence and trust in Me) has made you well! Go (enter) into peace (untroubled, undisturbed well-being).

Luke 8:43 –48 (AMP)

"You know what, Jenny? I've got one thing, and one thing only to say to you - if he isn't treating you *better* than I treat you, which is like a queen, then he isn't good enough for you. That's the bottom line."

Jenny quickly attempted to reply in her defence, but instead she paused for a second, stared out into nowhere, and pondered on her father's words.

"You know what, Paps... it's true. It's reaaaaally true."

"Jenny, for real, are you even listening?" I interjected. "I mean, you always *say* you get it, but *do* you?"

"I think I do, you know, Nat's," Jenny answered unconvincingly.

Trevor, looking mentally exhausted, rubbed his forehead before he continued. "Natalie... *please* talk to her."

I smiled back at Trevor... at this man who I'd always had so much respect for... and I felt humbled. It wasn't that long ago that I found myself listening to him speak to Jenny, while filled up with sadness and a twinge of resentment and jealousy, wishing that he was talking to *me*... wishing that I had such a loving and dedicated father. Who would've thought that years later I'd find myself being asked by Trevor to add to his words of wisdom? To say that God had brought me from a mighty long way was an understatement.

"Jen, you know what I think. We've gotta start thinking about our value. If we don't then we can't expect someone else to. I aint saying I'm all the way there yet, but I *do* know that if it was me in your situation and the guy wasn't aspiring to see and treat me the way God does, he would have to bounce. Simple."

Trevor smiled. Jenny sighed.

We'd both been trying to console and advise Jenny as she was contemplating her future with another "Gavin duplicate" who she was having relationship problems with. Although she'd finally split up with Gavin for good, she kept finding herself with guys *exactly* like him and kept wondering why she was getting the same results. She knew what she *needed* to do, but unfortunately it wasn't what she *wanted* to do. I could definitely relate.

After chilling at her parents house for the majority of the morning, both of our bellies rumbled, reminding us that it was lunchtime. As Jenny and I laughed at each other, deciding whose belly was rumbling the loudest, she received a timely text on her phone.

"Yes!! That's my girl," Jenny shrieked with excitement.

"Pleeeease tell me that's Esther ready with our food, 'cause I could mash up some hard food right about now?" I was hungry, enthusiastic, and in gleeful anticipation of Jenny's answer.

As Jenny grabbed her keys, kissed Trevor, yelled bye to her mum, and dashed towards the door, my question was answered. I didn't hang around either, and followed her in fast pursuit as Trevor teased us about our greediness.

We were on our way to Esther's. She'd opened up a small restaurant with Mark six months previously, and she was in her element. Getting the restaurant sorted out initially, and even making the decision to open it proved hard for her, but she finally decided to follow her heart and do what she'd always dreamt of doing. Her parents were still not one hundred per cent persuaded, but they were coming around to the idea. Jen and I were really happy for her and we still are.

By the time we arrived at the restaurant, Esther had already put our food aside and we sat down together outside and filled our bellies. We also couldn't help but laugh at Jenny who was struggling with her cutlery and chicken wings while Esther and I happily used our fingers.

It was a warm and sunny day in the middle of July, and after we'd eaten and our bellies had settled, there was that familiar awkward silence in the atmosphere. This had been happening for the last few years but particularly at this time of year. In fact, this same uncomfortable awkwardness frequently hovered around us when all three of us got together. We knew what we had to do that day, but it was still very raw and painful for us all.

"This is just so hard," Esther said quietly, breaking the silence.

Jenny and I remained silent. I looked at the empty spare chair at the table for four that we were sitting around, and it devastatingly reminded me that one of us was missing.

"Come, let's go and see her. It's a beautiful day, and I believe it's for her," Jenny said, trying to put on a brave face and hold back her tears.

As the three of us got into Jenny's car, Mark ran out of the restaurant to give us the flowers we forgot to bring outside, and we made our way to the cemetery to visit Shivon's grave.

Shivon had died of an overdose three years previously. She was never fully able to give up her hard partying and drug taking, which catapulted after her foster mum died of cancer. Sadly, a short while after that, Shivon's biological mum told her that she didn't want anything to do with her and asked her to not make contact with her again. To this day we don't know if the overdose was accidental or like the doctors concluded, but one thing I *do* know is that regardless of the circumstances, Shivon had always used drugs as a way of medicating her internal pain, and whether she intentionally killed herself or not, she did indeed - kill herself. That fact alone was just about enough for us all to deal with and none of us believed it was an accident. Only God knew. We missed her so much, and although we all remained close, our friendship with the absence of Shivon's laugh, love, presence, and irreplaceable personality could never ever be the same - and we all *knew* it.

We spent a long time at the cemetery that day reminiscing on the good times we shared with each other and tried to celebrate her by re-membering the best of her, but it was hard. I thought about her most days, but after thinking about her I was always left with a heavy feeling. As a Christian, I knew it was a sin to commit suicide and wondered what the eternal implications were if this was what Shivon had chosen; and even if that *wasn't* the case (to my knowledge) she hadn't given her life to the Lord. I desperately hoped that she was able to in her last moments alive or at some other time unbeknown to me.

People had a lot to say when she died like, *"Oh well, at least we know she's in a better place"*, and *"Well she lived her life to the fullest"* and other things like that, which I used to be guilty of saying myself. But what did that mean exactly? Was that the truth or was it just what people chose to say to make themselves feel better about the person's passing? Either way, this was my experience. It was what I did, what I saw, and was also the behaviour of most people around me.

The reality is that when somebody dies, and once all of their fun and living it up and doing what they want to do is over, we as their family and friends find ourselves sitting in a church dedicating this person's body back to the dust from whence they came. Many times it's *only* at *this* point that we want to get sentimental or think about anything relating to divinity or eternity. No one usually wants to think about eternity until these things happen, which is a serious issue because let's face it - eternity is a *long* time. No one wants to ask the one and only question that matters at this point and that is: Where is this person's soul? Did they know and have a relationship with Jesus Christ? I appreciate that it's too uncomfortable for people to go there, it certainly was for me, but why avoid the unavoidable?

1Thessalonians 4: 13-18 says: *"And now, dear brothers and sisters, we want you to know what will happen to the believers who have died so you will not grieve like people who have no hope. For since we believe that Jesus died and was raised to life again, we also believe that when Jesus returns, God will bring back with him the believers who have died. We tell you this directly from the Lord: We who are still living when the Lord returns will not meet him ahead of those who have died. For the Lord himself will come down from heaven with a commanding shout, with the voice of the archangel, and with the trumpet call of God. First, the Christians who have died will rise from their graves. Then, together with them, we who are still alive and remain on the earth will be caught up in the clouds to meet the Lord in the air. Then we will be with the Lord forever. So encourage each other with these words"*.

These words encouraged me when Sister Stewart died. When Shivon died, I didn't feel encouraged... I didn't feel comforted... all I had was hope. All I knew to be true was that it was *my* responsibility to seek the Lord while He may be found and to call on Him while He is near (Isaiah 55:6), and this was exactly what I was trying to do.

After a very reflective day, we went back to my house after picking up Daniel and reflected some more. I loved my girlies and although none of us had arrived, it was clear that we were all on our own individual journey. Jenny had finally begun to wear less make up and had slowly begun to feel more comfortable in her own skin. Her relationship with Joel was still a bit strained, but it was a whole lot better than it had been. Jenny had also started to come to Sarah's house with me every now and again, and I was hoping and praying that God would continue to lavish His love on her and that her heart would be receptive. Esther and Mark began to attend Mark's grandmother's church and were planning their wedding. Their son

Justin and my big boy Daniel were growing up really well and they remained very close friends. Daniel was also doing great in school, and as for me... well I had gone on to begin and successfully finish the postgraduate programme just as I planned to do after my three years of studying dance. I struggled harder than I could've imagined when Shivon died and wanted to give up on my studying, but I pushed through for her, for me, for Daniel, and for the gratitude I had to God for putting me in that position in the first place. I had a few ideas of what I wanted to do with my qualifications, but took a few years out from any intense work schedules or extra study to spend more time with my son and to grow in my walk with Christ. Merely existing was a thing of the past and it was all down to the power, love, and grace of the one true God - Jesus Christ.

When Jenny and Esther went home that night I sat in my bed in tears over the amount of ups and downs that had occurred over the last few years. So much had happened and God had brought me through so much that I almost didn't recognise myself.

As I sat in bed that evening feeling a little bit peckish, I wondered what I could treat myself to after having my little cry. Daniel had fallen asleep and I was secretly happy about that. Sometimes, I just didn't want to share certain treats with Daniel. His appetite was growing as quickly as he was.

While I pondered on what to eat, I reached for my bible and read the story of the woman with the issue of blood, who Jesus healed after her many trips to physicians who could not help her. I thought about all of my "physicians"; weed, sex, work, college, men, and everything else. I thought about the things that still needed to be worked out in my character, thankful that God could do it with my obedience. I thought about Jenny's obsession with make up and over achieving, and Esther's people-pleasing nature due to rejection. I thought about all of our other self - harming traits and wondered how grieved God must be. I knew that all He wanted to do was to fill the gap that was designed for only Him to fill. All He wanted was for us to be fully restored and in a right relationship with Him; back to His original plan of how it should've been in the first place. I also thought about how readily available the choice was.

I smiled in blissful anticipation about my future and the future of those around me. I sighed... smiled again... and closed my eyes and said a simple prayer that went something like this:

"Thank you for *everything*, Jesus. Thank you for taking my brokenness and blessing me. You are without a shadow of a doubt, the one and only TRUE physician."

After that, I reached over to turn off my bedside lamp and went to sleep... but not without going back downstairs for a scoop of vanilla ice cream first. Of course the ice cream wasn't a touch on Nenna's... but it was close ☺ .

I once thought these things were valuable, but now I consider them worthless because of what Christ has done. Yes, everything else is worthless when compared with the infinite value of knowing Christ Jesus my Lord. For His sake I have discarded everything else, counting it all as garbage, so that I could gain Christ and become one with him.

Philippians 3:7-9 (NLT)

The fool says in his heart "There is no God".

Psalm 14:1 (NIV)

They know the truth about God because He has made it obvious to them. For ever since the world was created, people have seen the earth and sky. Through everything God made, they can clearly see His invisible qualities—His eternal power and divine nature. So they have no excuse for not knowing God.

Romans 1:19-20 (NLT)

ABOUT THE AUTHOR

Verona Marshall has been passionate about expressing herself through writing, ever since she was a young child. She first discovered her gift and love for writing when she started her first journal at 9 years old. Verona is the visionary and leader of I Am Woman, a ministry designed to equip and empower young mothers to become all they were created to be, and to provide them with a platform to be heard and valued. She has also spent a number of years as a Young Mothers Support Co Ordinator by profession, and is the mother of 2 beautiful girls.